Mungo can hardly believe mum asking Aunt Janet if she will look after him for a month. He knows that Aunt Janet hates him as much as he hates her, and there's nothing in the world that will make him spend a whole month at her house, especially after all the things she's said about his dad, whose extravagant and fun-loving ways have finally landed him in prison. No, there's just one thing to do and that's to get away, leave his friends and family behind for a month and head north on the open road with his freedom machine. His freedom machine is a bike called Gulliver, and he's Mungo's great friend and companion. Together they set off very early one morning on their great adventure heading for freedom.

Mungo learns many things about himself and other people on his journey and soon realizes that his freedom isn't quite what he'd expected.

Joan Lingard was born in Edinburgh but grew up in Belfast, where she lived until she was eighteen. She is the author of the Sadie and Kevin novels about modern Belfast and *Frying as Usual*, which are all published in Puffin. She has three grown-up daughters and lives in Edinburgh with her Canadian husband.

The Freedom Machine

by
JOAN LINGARD

PUFFIN BOOKS

PUFFIN BOOKS

Published by the Penguin Group
27 Wrights Lane, London W8 5TZ, England
Viking Penguin Inc., 40 West 23rd Street, New York, New York 10010, USA
Penguin Books Australia Ltd, Ringwood, Victoria, Australia
Penguin Books Canada Ltd, 2801 John Street, Markham, Ontario, Canada L3R 1B4
Penguin Books (NZ) Ltd, 182–190 Wairau Road, Auckland 10, New Zealand

Penguin Books Ltd, Registered Offices: Harmondsworth, Middlesex, England

First published by Hamish Hamilton Children's Books 1986
Published in Puffin Books 1988
3 5 7 9 10 8 6 4

Made and printed in Great Britain by
Richard Clay Ltd, Bungay, Suffolk

Contents

For Russell
with love

1

Countdown

Some people think it's daft to talk to a bicycle but I don't see why. There are some people who might as well be doors or windows when you speak to them for all the attention they pay. They don't even seem to hear what you're saying. That's what my mum was like the few days before I took off on my freedom machine.

My freedom machine is my bike and he's called Gulliver. Yes — he. Why shouldn't it be called he? He's my pal. It was my dad who called him a freedom machine. He loves cycling himself, not that he's doing much at the moment. But I'm not going to think about that just now, I definitely am not.

My dad used to say that when he got on his bike he felt he could go anywhere in the world — he felt free. We used to go for long rides into the country on Sunday mornings, he and I. We'd set out before anyone else was up and the street was dead quiet. My mum stayed at home with the twins. They're both girls, and only five years old, and they ride three-wheeled tricycles up and down the pavement getting in everybody's way.

"One of these days," my dad said when the twins were complaining about being left behind, "we'll all go out into the country together on big bikes."

One of these days. I was thinking about that the evening before Gulliver and I set off on our travels. The day couldn't be for at least three years, if ever. As far as I was concerned it would be never. In three years' time I'd be thirteen and by then I wouldn't care about my father at all. It was at that moment that I started thinking about him as my father, not my dad any more.

The doorbell rang.

"Go see who that is," said my mum, who was ironing. She always seems to be ironing, or washing. The twins go through an awful lot of clothes. They're good at walking into puddles and getting oil on their jeans from tricycle chains.

I opened the front door of our flat and there on the landing stood Pete, my best friend. Apart from Gulliver, that is. The thing is Gulliver's *always* there when you want him. Pete was leaning against the bannister rail, half hanging over it backwards. He was lucky my mum couldn't see him.

"Hi!" he said. "Coming out?"

"Dunno," I shrugged.

"Aw, come on, Mungo."

"Yes, why don't you?" said my mum, who had come to see who it was. "Do you good to get some fresh air." Usually she has a job to get me in. Then she turned her attention to Pete.

"How many times do you boys have to be told not to lean over the bannisters? Do you want to fall into the stair well and break your necks?"

He straightened himself up.

"Go on now, Mungo," said my mum. "You're getting on my nerves, anyway, fidgeting about the kitchen. Like a hen on a hot griddle."

I didn't bother to reply to that one. I followed Pete down the stairs.

"Your mother's fairly got her knickers in a twist tonight." I didn't bother to reply to that, either. I'd be glad when Gulliver and I did finally take off.

He was standing in the bottom passage, his shiny racing green paint gleaming even in the dim light. I'd padlocked the back wheel and fixed the frame to the railing with a chain when I came in earlier. You can't afford to take any chances round here with the bicycle thieves that are going about. Pete had his bike nicked but he didn't mind too much. He got a better one on the Insurance. But I could never get a better bike than Gulliver.

"You're darned right you couldn't." (When he speaks I'm the only one who can hear him.)

I patted his saddle as we went by.

"Won't be long now, Gully," I said to him inside my head. "You can start the countdown."

Billy and Mike were out in the street knocking a ball about.

"How's your father?" asked Billy.

"Lay off!" said Pete and aimed a kick at his ankle.

Billy dodged sideways and missed it but he didn't say any more on the subject of my father. He'd said enough in the past month.

"Have a gum?" Mike pulled out half a packet of wine

fruit gums. They tasted of turpentine. He often has turpentiny rags in his pocket. His father's a painter and decorator. We ate the gums anyway.

We roamed about the streets for a while and then drifted down to the river. It's a bit scummy at times and there are often things floating in it, empty packets and stuff, but we like it down there. Big trees with thick branches hang over it.

"We should have brought our fishing rods," said Pete.

I nodded. We both like fishing. Not that we ever catch very much, only the odd minnow and it's just as likely to be an old boot.

We sat on the bank and watched the water birling along and the birds flitting under the low hanging branches. It was almost as good as being in the country, though not quite, for there was always the sound of traffic when you listened and you knew that when you walked along the path to the bridge you'd be back in the busy street again. I'd like to live in the country, but my mum wouldn't. She'd miss her friends and the second-hand shops that she's forever rummaging in. My father grew up in the country, ran wild on the hills, fished, milked cows, helped bring in the hay. And now —

"Let's go," I said.

We drifted back to the street where we hung about on the corner and I guess we were making a bit of a noise.

"Can't you find something else to do?" muttered old man Cassidy as he went by carrying his fish supper. The smell made my mouth water.

"Get lost!" Bill shouted after him. His mother, who

4

calls him William, doesn't like him hanging about in our street (or shouting after old men). She'd prefer him to sit at home in their nice clean bungalow reading the encyclopaedias she buys from the men who call at the door. When he takes us home we have to leave our shoes on the back step and his mother spreads newspapers on the settee before she lets us sit down.

"Fancy some chips?" asked Billy. "I've got money."

"I'm going in," I said.

"See you tomorrow," said Pete.

I nodded, though I knew I wouldn't.

"I'll ring your bell," he said and ran off to catch up with the others.

I hadn't even been able to tell Pete about my plans. I'd told nobody but Gulliver. He was the only one I could trust to keep his mouth shut! I told him so when I came back into the lobby.

"I'm glad you appreciate me," he said. "Just as well, considering the time I have to spend hanging about here waiting for you. And don't sleep in!" he called after me. "I know you, Mungo McKinnon!"

I didn't intend to sleep at all.

"You're back early," said my mother, looking up from the sink where she was rinsing sheets. Her washing machine was broken and she said the launderette was too dear.

I didn't say anything. For the last few days I'd found it difficult to speak to her at all.

"Want some supper?"

I wasn't particularly hungry but I made myself a cup of hot chocolate and ate a slice of bread with peanut butter. I had to keep my strength up. And I was glad to get the turpentiny-gum taste out of my mouth.

While I was eating my mother went on rinsing and sluicing and squeezing, taking longer than she needed, or so it seemed to me. She hadn't had much to say to me recently, either. She was going to speak to me tomorrow.

"I'll tell him on Saturday," I'd heard her say to my Aunt Janet. Overheard. I'd stood in the passage with my ear pressed against the wall trying to make out what they were saying. They'd kept their voices down so that I wasn't able to catch every word. But I'd caught enough.

2

Take Off

"I'm off to bed," I said and got up.

"Goodnight then, love." My mother turned round from the sink. I avoided her eye. "You're not getting a cold or anything?"

"No. Why?"

"You sound a bit gruff, that's all."

"I'm fine."

I didn't kiss her goodnight and I saw that she was hurt. As she put her back to me again her head drooped over the sink. But somehow I just couldn't kiss her, not that night.

"Look after your mother," my father had said to me. But what right did he have to tell me what to do? He hadn't made much of a job of looking after her himself. My throat felt tight as if it were being pulled together inside with strings and I wondered if I might be coming down with a cold after all. Or perhaps beri-beri or yellow fever. I felt peculiar enough for anything.

I made for the door and I didn't look back. I went straight to my bedroom.

It was full of heat after a long day of sunshine. It's not a proper room, just a boxroom with a skylight. Our flat's only got two bedrooms and the twins sleep in the second one.

7

I climbed on to the bed to push the window further up and stood for a few minutes on the saggy old mattress looking out at the sky. It was still a deep blue and there were a few faint stars just beginning to show. I found the evening star. On a summer night like this it wouldn't be dark until after eleven, and it would be light again by four. I'd be away by then.

I got back down, and although I had no intention of sleeping, put on my pyjamas. Lying stretched out in bed I checked my stores over again in my head in case I'd forgotten anything. They were all ready to go underneath the bed.

In my red rucksack I'd packed a spare tee-shirt, two pairs of socks, a pair of underpants, a sweater, a woollen hat (it might get cold at nights), a tin of plasters, a tube of antiseptic cream, my clasp knife, a tin opener, a torch (with a spare battery), a box of matches, some tin foil, a bar of soap, an old towel, a roll of loo paper, a notebook and biro, two maps, a small tin of black paint, a brush, a book on mushrooms and one of crossword puzzles, and *Gulliver's Travels*. It was a children's version of the book and had once been my father's. He gave it to me after I named my bike. My Gulliver likes the idea of being a giant amongst midgets. Sometimes I read aloud to him about the other Gulliver's adventures in the land of Lilliput.

My door was being opened very quietly. The hinges squeaked. A shaft of light fell across my bed, just missing my face. I closed my eyes. My mother came tiptoeing into the room, pausing after every step to see if I was asleep. I could hear her breathing. She tucked the covers in round my shoulders and then she bent over to kiss me goodnight. Her soft hair fell across my cheek and I smelt the lemony smell of the shampoo that she uses. That was kind of difficult, that moment. In fact, it was very difficult. I almost put up my arm to hold her there but I stopped myself, just in time. For I knew that if I did I'd never get away. I knew that I'd tell her what I had planned to do. I knew that I'd tell her how worried I was about her. So, instead, I concentrated on breathing more deeply and felt my chest rising and falling.

She tiptoed out again and the door closed behind her.

The luminous dial of my watch said five to eleven. My mum wouldn't go to bed for another hour or so; she'd potter about doing chores, putting off the moment of going into her room. Some mornings she looked all in, as if she hadn't slept at all.

I pushed her to the back of my mind — I had to if I was going to stick to my plan — and went back to checking my stores. Beside the rucksack was my sleeping bag, rolled up, ready to be tied to the back of Gulliver's seat, and a bag of food which I was going to put into the paniers when I went downstairs.

The food consisted of dates (three packets), which I knew that climbers took when they went on the hills, nuts and raisins (again three packets), two apples, two bananas, two oranges, a packet of digestive biscuits, a bottle of orange juice, two bars of chocolate and two rolls filled with cheese and two with ham. Not enough to last a month, of course! I would need to buy some as well.

In my drawer I had seven pounds which I'd been saving towards a track suit. And some food, like berries and mushrooms, I could get for free. We used to go mushroom-picking, my father and I, on damp mornings when the mist was still hovering over the fields.

My mum seemed to be going to bed at last. I heard the clink of the milk bottles as she put them out on the landing and the door being snibbed and then she went into the bathroom. Finally, the door of her room clicked shut.

A church clock in the next street chimed out twelve times. It was hot. I kicked off the bedcovers. And now Cathy, one of the twins, cried out, but before my mum could get up and see to her she quietened again.

The clock struck one. A terrible cramp suddenly seized up my left leg. It was as if my calf had got caught in a vice and was being squeezed hard. I almost cried out with the fierceness of it and had to sit up in bed and massage the muscle frantically until the blood came back into it and the pain seeped away. I lay back exhausted.

And then I must have fallen asleep, for the next thing I knew the room was bright as day and I could see sunshine through the skylight. I leapt up. It was five o'clock!

"Damn," I said to myself, very, very quietly. "*Damn!*"

I felt like banging my head against the wall I was so annoyed with myself. I had to make do with giving it a good scratch. If things had gone according to plan I would have been well away by this time, on the other side of the Forth road bridge heading north. Now I would have to make my getaway in broad daylight.

Getting dressed, I felt as if I had five thumbs on each hand. I buckled the straps of my rucksack up squint. The drawer grated when I opened it to get my money out. I was sure everyone in the house would have been wakened by the noise. For a moment I stayed quite still, listening. I could hear my heart beating. Boom, boom, boom. It sounded like a drum.

Slinging the rucksack over one shoulder, I clamped the sleeping bag into my armpit and took the paniers in that hand, leaving the other one free to open doors. I had to be careful that I didn't bang the rucksack against the door frame as I edged my way round. My mother coughed. I stopped again. Then, holding my breath, I made it into the kitchen.

In my jeans pocket I had an envelope. It had got a bit creased so I straightened it out before I propped it up on the mantelpiece against the clock. Wasn't that where people were supposed to leave notes?

'Don't worry,' I'd written. 'Please don't worry. I shall be okay. Take care of yourself and get well soon.'

Sun was pouring into the kitchen. It might have been midday. I took a last look round and left.

As I was unsnibbing the flat door Cathy said in a clear voice, "Susie, are you awake?"

I didn't wait to hear if Susie was, I opened the door quickly and in a flash was on the other side and running down the three flights of stairs to where Gulliver was waiting for me.

"I told you not to fall asleep, didn't I?"

"All right, all right! No point in going on."

Working fast, not fumbling any more, I released him from his chains and locks and fixed the paniers and sleeping bag into place. The rucksack I hoisted up on to my back. I tugged the heavy old door open and wheeled Gulliver out into the street. There was nothing else moving, not even a cat.

With a leap I was up into the saddle and we went bumping down from the pavement on to the road. We were off!

I cut through small streets to the Queensferry Road. It would take us to the Forth road bridge which spans the wide Firth of Forth. Before it was built twenty-five years ago people had to cross the water by ferry. It was called the Queen's Ferry after Queen Margaret, who lived in the eleventh century and was married to a king called Malcolm Canmore. My father had told me that and it was as if he were telling me again now. I could hear his voice inside my head and I didn't want to hear it ever again.

"Shut up!" I said and turned my head to see if anyone was about to hear.

There was only a milk float. The driver gave me a wave as he passed. He didn't seem to think it at all odd that a boy of my age should be out on the road so early in the morning. Not that it was *that* early any more and the milkman had probably been up for hours. The milk boy, who was sitting on the back of the float swinging his legs, looked at me with more curiosity and he didn't wave. Both he and the man, if they were to read about me in the paper the next day, might remember me but I couldn't do anything about that.

There's nothing special about me though, so at least that was something. I look pretty much like any other ten year old boy. My hair is brown and so are my eyes and my build is middling, neither skinny like Pete's nor heavy like Billy's. Now if it had been Pete he would have stood out, for apart from being as thin as a rake he's the tallest boy in the class and he has hair the colour of burnt carrots.

The milk float turned into a side road and was gone. There was no one in front of me at all now. I took a quick look over my shoulder to see if all was clear to the rear as well.

It was then that I saw the police car coming up behind me.

3

Into the Kingdom of Fife

Gulliver's back wheel did a bit of a wobble and we swerved.

"Steady on there!" he cried. "Keep the heid!"

I soon had myself, and him, under control again and, putting my head down, I pushed hard on the pedals.

"Not too fast now," said Gulliver, "or they'll think you're running away."

"Smart Alec!" I said, but I slackened off a little. The sound of the police car grew louder. Was its blue light flashing? Would its siren start screaming any minute now? It couldn't be after me, I told myself, it couldn't, for my mum wouldn't be up yet and even if she were she wouldn't have had time to do anything.

The car drew level. The policeman on the passenger side glanced out at me in a casual sort of way. He didn't seem much interested but you could never be sure which way a policeman was looking at you and perhaps he would make a note in his head. Boy on a green bike . . .

Anyway, I was going to change that. The black paint in my rucksack would wipe out the green.

"You won't like that, will you, Gully?"

"Certainly not!"

"Nor will I. But we've got to do everything we can to throw people off our track."

The police car was streaming away far up ahead now and vanishing fast into the distance.

"We can relax, Gully."

The only other vehicle to pass us for a while was a rackety old van, puffing horrible gunk out from its exhaust pipe. The man and woman in front seemed to be having an argument and didn't look the side I was on.

Gradually more cars began to appear, some with holiday luggage tied to their roofs, and soon, showing against the skyline, came the three humps of the Forth railway bridge. My father used to say they reminded him of the Loch Ness monster when he saw them standing out in the mist or at dusk.

"Oh, do shut up!" I cried.

"Hear, hear!" said Gulliver.

It was bright and clear for miles around, with no trace of mist to blur either of the two bridges. I headed straight for the road one and was glad to see that a car was approaching the toll booth nearest the cycle and foot passenger track. It would take the attendant's eyes away from me. I put on an extra spurt and went flying on to the bridge. Cyclists travel free.

I love the feeling of cycling high up over the water but that morning I couldn't quite enjoy anything, not yet, not until I would be well away up north, far from the Edinburgh area. I gave a quick thought to Queen Margaret and imagined her being rowed across the water below me in a small boat. History's my favourite subject and Margaret's my favourite queen because that's my mum's name too.

At the thought of my mum I had to gulp to get rid of the lump in my throat. I knew that what I was doing to her was pretty mean but what else could I do? *What else?*

"Nothing," said Gulliver.

My mum should still be in bed. It was only half-past six and she seldom gets up before eight. The twins, if they were awake, would have gone into the kitchen and helped themselves to muesli, leaving a mess all over the kitchen table which usually I have to clear up, and then they'd go back to bed and play. They're lucky, they have one another, they're never on their own. Though my mum says there are drawbacks to being twins. Being together all the time makes them not bother about other friends. Or their brother! They just seem to think I'm a slave whose job it is to clear up behind them.

'I am going to go and stay somewhere safe,' I had written in the letter to my mum. 'So there is no need for you to send the police after me. *Please don't.*'

She wasn't likely to pay any attention to that but I counted on her not going to the police straightaway. She'd read my letter over another couple of times and then go downstairs in her dressing gown to see if Gulliver was missing and after that she'd come back up and make a pot of tea and read the letter yet again and sit and think. I know how her mind works.

The next move would be to call her sister. "I'll be straight over, Margaret," Aunt Janet would say. She usually comes over for a powwow when anything is up. She came at the double the day my father was arrested.

"I can't say I'm completely surprised," she had said,

as she plonked herself down in the armchair by the fire. "Oh, I don't mean that I ever thought he would do anything *criminal* — but he *was* extravagant, wasn't he?"

No one could accuse Aunt Janet or her husband Uncle Eddie of extravagance. They budget everything carefully, so much for food and so much for bus fares, and live well within their means. Aunt Janet is always talking about living within your means and cutting your coat according to your cloth, and when she does I imagine her with a huge pair of scissors and a tiny bit of cloth. She'd often talk like that in front of my father, meaning it to be a kind of warning, but it would just make him laugh. When she'd gone he'd say, "Those two don't know how to let go once in a while and enjoy themselves — that's their trouble!"

He'd known how to enjoy himself only too well — that had been *his* trouble.

The end of the bridge was coming up. We zoomed off and were back on the road. We were now in the ancient Kingdom of Fife. Kingdom! I liked the sound of that. It was like arriving in another country. No one knows for sure why it's called a kingdom but it has been for centuries. My father thinks it was probably a Pictish kingdom.

Shortly afterwards, we turned off on to a secondary road. We had to leave the main road north there as it becomes a motorway at this point and bicycles aren't allowed on that, but we'd rejoin it again after Perth when it goes back to being an ordinary highway.

I planned to ride for another three hours before I took a break. I reckoned that it would take my mum and aunt until after ten to chew it all over and go round and ask Pete and Mike and Billy if they knew anything. Pete's mother would ask them in and so would Mike's, but Billy's wouldn't. She'd keep them standing on the step and she'd twitch her nose to one side as if there was a nasty smell somewhere in the area. She didn't like her William having anything to do with a convict's family. He had told me so and I had told him that my father was innocent, he'd been framed.

"Liar!"

"It's the truth, I tell you!"

"He didn't do it, did he, Mum?" I asked her when I went home from school that afternoon.

"I'm afraid he did, love."

"Well, I'm not going back to school and you can't make me!"

She did, of course. By talking about the attendance officer and the trouble he could cause for her and didn't she have enough problems already? And then I might have to go before the Children's Panel and they could take me away from her. They might say she couldn't cope.

"And nuisance that you are, I wouldn't want that to happen!"

Back at school I got into one or two fights, though not with Billy, for he might be big but he doesn't like fighting. Nor do I for that matter. But sometimes it just seems to start and before you know it you're in there too. My mum says that's not a good enough excuse. Billy always shouts his taunts from a distance and as soon as it looks like there might be trouble he's off.

"Pay no attention," said Pete. "He doesn't mean it. He just gabs a lot."

Like Aunt Janet. Boy, can she gab!

"I don't know, Margaret," she had said after my father was found guilty and sent to prison, "but I don't see why you should stand by him. After all, he's broken the law. He is a criminal."

"Of course I'll stand by him! Anyway, he did it for us."

"He did it because he was in debt. Up to his ears." Aunt Janet sounded almost pleased when she said that. I suppose she thought that if you saved your money for bus fares you'd never end up in jail.

"Been to visit your dad?" Billy asked every morning in the playground before school started. "Is he kept behind bars? Like a chimp?" And he capered about looking more like a clumsy baboon. My mother asked me why I bothered with him when he was so nasty and I never quite knew the answer to that. It was just that he was around and we'd always hung out in the same gang.

I was glad when the last day of term came. The teacher called me back as we were going out. She wanted a word with me.

"Mungo, I know this has been a difficult time for you but by next term they'll all have got used to it and they'll lay off."

I knew, though, that *I* would never get used to it. I

dodged my pals and ran home. Aunt Janet was in the kitchen, I heard her as soon as I opened the flat door. She was saying, "Money always did burn a hole in his pocket." She can repeat the same things over and over again without seeming to get bored. "I mean to say, Margaret, he'd take you all out for meals and then there was that bike he bought for Mungo. Well, he couldn't really afford it, could he? He's always spoiled that boy."

The bike was one of the best makes on the market and it had ten gears. I was glad of them now. Good old Gully! We went steaming up hills almost as easily as we sailed down them. I felt the breeze in my hair and the sun on my face and as I pedalled I forgot for a while all the people I'd left behind. I began to enjoy the ride.

"Why not enjoy it?" said Gully. "I am."

4

A Quiet Spot

Cars were passing us more often now. On such a fine summer day, and with the schools on holiday, there was bound to be a lot of traffic on the road by lunchtime. I would not stay on it myself until then. I would find a quiet spot and lie low. Even though I was keeping in close to the edge I felt quite jittery when a truck came thundering up behind me. I was glad to see it pass. Its wheels were so large! In comparison, Gulliver's were tiny.

"Not *too* tiny," he growled.

A stream of cyclists went by, their heads bent low over their handlebars, their eyes fixed on the strip of road in front of them. The looked very serious. They were travelling much faster than we were. I made a big effort and tried to keep up with them but they were older and I suppose more experienced and the distance between us and them widened. I was flagging.

"So what?" said Gulliver. "We're doing all right."

By ten o'clock I was whacked out and my tummy complaining. I stopped at the side for a moment and looked at the map. We must have been well over half way to Perth which was our destination for the night. I took the next side turning off the road and was glad to leave its noise and busyness behind. We were in real country now and I could hear the birds.

"This is more like it, isn't it, Gully?"

"Sure is. Much more."

I pulled him up on a bridge which straddled an old railway embankment. It looked cool underneath the bridge and it would be a nice tucked-away kind of place to hole up in for a while. I scrambled down the bank, helping Gully over the rough ground.

I parked him in the shade and squatted beside him. The single track was completely overgrown and the sleepers had been pulled up a long time ago. It would have been a branch line linking small villages to one another in the days when trains puffed their way all over the country, stopping at neat little stations with flowers blooming in boxes along the platforms. I imagined a train going through right in front of us with its whistle blowing, its paintwork shining, smoke billowing from its funnel, and all the people leaning out of their carriages to wave to Gulliver and me. My father said it was a scandal that the railways had been hacked about in the way they had, it showed that folk didn't think about the future when they did something (had *he*?) and now the roads were getting busier and busier every year.

"Oh, why can't you just *keep quiet*?" I shouted aloud.

"Cool it," said Gulliver. "Why don't you just have your breakfast?"

First I ate a ham roll. I'd never tasted anything so good. Then I had a cheese one and half a bar of chocolate and after that I drank an inch of orange juice. I took my time, letting each drop slide over my throat. It felt as if a sandstorm had swept through it. Getting enough liquid was going to be a problem, but further north there would be burns I could drink from so I let myself have another half-inch. I would have to be careful, though, about food and drink and ration myself strictly. I looked at the dates, began to open the packet and then decided better not. Before I'd be tempted any more I put them and the rest of the food back in the panier and took out the paint and brush.

A big yawn took me over for a moment. I could hardly keep my eyes open. I would paint Gulliver and then while he was drying I would lie back and sleep for a while. The promise of that pushed me on.

"Poor old Gully! Sorry about this. But it'll only be for a month. That's not long, is it?"

"Long enough when you've got to go around not looking like yourself."

In fact, four weeks did seem quite long. They stretched away into the distance like forever, only I didn't want to say that to Gulliver. We had to survive for that length of time and afterwards we would go back home. By then my mother would have got over her operation. She *would* get over it.

"She'll be all right, won't she, Gully?" I said and felt really miserable.

"Sure she will," he said cheerfully. "She's strong, your mum. And it's a good hospital."

"I'll be in hospital for about ten days, Janet," she'd said to my aunt, "and then they want me to go to a convalescent home. They say I musn't come straight back and start running the house again. They say it wouldn't give me a proper chance."

The two of them might well be on their way to the police station by now, my mum saying shouldn't they wait a bit longer? She always prefers to wait, Aunt Janet doesn't. "What's the point in wasting time?" She would lead the way forward.

"What are you going to do about it then, Officer?" she would demand, parking her elbows on the counter. My father said it would have been better if she'd had children of her own, it would have left her less time to stick her nose into other people's business. Once, when she was getting up my nose telling me what to do — "Why don't you join the Cubs, Mungo, or the Boys' Brigade, it would give you something useful to do instead of hanging round the street annoying folk?" — I turned round and told her what my father had said.

Well, after that, she and I never got on at all, so I wasn't surprised when I heard her telling my mum she wasn't one bit keen on the idea of taking me in along with the twins for a month, but if no other arrangement could be made then she'd just have to. She knew where her duty lay.

"What about that Pete boy he's so pally with?" she asked. "I thought you said they were as thick as thieves? Sorry, Margaret, I shouldn't have said that, should I? I mean, under the circumstances . . . . But would Pete's mother not have him?"

"I don't like to ask. Not when it's for a month. And

there are five children in his family. I wish I didn't have to ask *you*, Janet." My mother sounded miserable then. "But there's nothing else I can do. All my friends have got more than enough on their plates."

"And I don't?"

"Well, I know you have your afternoon job but Mrs Sweeney next door has offered — "

"But I don't have any children, that's what you mean, isn't it? Not like all your friends who have so many they might as well be living in shoes. It amazes me how they can afford it. Don't think until it's too late, I suppose." Aunt Janet had forgotten about keeping her voice down and was warming up to another lecture about scissors and cloth. I didn't stay to listen. I slipped into my bedroom and began making my plans, for I knew one thing for sure — that nothing in the whole world would make me stay for a month with Aunt Janet.

My mum used to tell me that her sister meant well; but I was fed up with people like Aunt Janet and Billy who were supposed to 'mean well' and yet said horrible things as if they couldn't keep them from spilling out of their mouths. If Aunt Janet believed so much in the self-control she was always going on about surely she could have learnt to keep her own tongue in check by this time.

"What about getting on with the painting?" said Gulliver. "I don't fancy being half-green and half-black. Would you?"

I had finished his frame and was beginning on the rear mudguard when I heard a voice overhead.

"What are you doing, lad?" it asked.

5

Once a Thief

I looked up to see an upside-down face staring at me. It was fringed with hair the colour of steel wool — hair which stuck out in all directions.

"What are you up to?" asked the round hole that was the mouth. There didn't seem to be many teeth in it, from what I could see. But I couldn't see all that well because of the funny angle it was at.

"You'll get dizzy," I said.

The head swung up and away from me and for a moment moved out of my sight. Then a pair of boots without laces appeared on the bank and a pair of legs in flapping trousers and the trunk of a body trussed up in what looked like several coats and waistcoats, and finally, the head again, right side up.

"You must be sweltered," I said, "on a day like this."

"Winter, summer," he said, "I wear the same."

He slithered down the rest of the bank and came to join me under the hump of the bridge. His smell made me inch away a little but he didn't seem to notice. He put down the plastic bag he was carrying and settled himself comfortably.

"A bit of shade doesn't come amiss, though." He eyed Gulliver. "You never answered my question, lad."

26

"I'm painting my bike," I said and took up where I'd left off.

He watched me for a while, then asked, "What's your name?" I hoped he wasn't going to ask too many questions.

I thought for a moment before answering. "James." There didn't seem much chance of him going to the police but you couldn't be sure. And James *was* my second name. "What's yours?"

"Rupert."

"Rupert?"

"That's right."

I had been about to say that it didn't seem a very likely name for a tramp but stopped myself. He might not like being called a tramp — my father said they regarded themselves as gentlemen of the road. And I didn't know what kind of names tramps would be called. I hadn't really got into conversation with one before. There are always a few hanging about in the centre of Edinburgh and one often picks through the garbage in our street along with the other bucket-rakers.

"They don't do any harm," says my mother. "And if they can make use of what we throw out, good luck to them!"

"Got anything to drink?" asked Rupert.

"No beer or anything like that."

"Anything at all?" A furred-looking tongue came out and snaked around the hairy lips. "Haven't had a drink yet today."

I hesitated. Well, I didn't much fancy him drinking

from my bottle. Who would? Pete and I would drink from the same bottle but we're friends, we know one another and we're more or less clean. You couldn't have said Rupert was. And he might have all sorts of horrible germs which I wasn't too fussy about catching, especially since I was going to be living rough for a month.

"I've a terrible thirst on me," he said. "And you're a kind-looking boy."

"Oh, all right."

I took out my bottle of orange juice and passed it to him. He put it to his mouth and tipped his head back. The juice went glugging down his throat. When he'd finished, he wiped his mouth with the back of his hand which was covered by a half-mitten, and passed back the bottle. I took it though I knew I would not drink the rest of the juice. I cursed myself. That had been stupid of me. I had a terrible thirst on me too.

"Anything to eat?" he asked next.

"I suppose you're starving?"

"Right."

I offered him a date, which *I* broke off from the others, but he didn't fancy that.

"Haven't you got any sandwiches or anything?"

I gave him the remaining ham one.

"God bless you, son!"

I fastened the panier. He was getting nothing more.

"Where are you going, lad?"

"North. To visit some relatives."

He sat chewing and thinking so I decided it would be

better if I turned the tables and started putting some questions to him. I asked where he was going.

"I'm never going anywhere in particular like. I just goes around. Where the fancy takes me. I sleeps in barns and under hedges and bridges. Depending on the weather."

I was curious.

"Were you unemployed? Was that why you became a tramp?"

"I suppose you could say that."

"Do you like being one?"

"I'd call it being a traveller more, lad. There's no other life I'd have. Winter I goes into Edinburgh and stays some nights in the hostel but in the mornings I can't wait to get out of the place. Can't stand houses. Can't stand walls round me."

I wondered if I travelled for long enough would I come to feel like that, too? But when winter came I thought I'd probably want to go back indoors and sit by the fire and drink hot chocolate and eat hot toast. I kind of liked the idea, though, of travelling and going where you fancied.

"Did you always hate houses?"

"No. Once I used to live in one."

"Why did you change your mind?"

"I was sent to prison, you see."

"Prison?" I felt as if hot blood was rushing madly through my head. "What for?"

"I stole some money. Quite a lot, in fact." He chuckled. "Fat lot of good it did me. Before I'd time to spend it they got hold of me."

"How long were you in prison for?"

"Four years. When I came out I took to the hills and wandered about like a daft thing. From then on I couldn't stomach four walls round me again. I was a bank clerk. Can you imagine it, lad, me in a bank?"

I couldn't, no matter how hard I tried. I stared at the battered-looking face and the bloodshot eyes and the stubbly hair that bristled all over his chin and I couldn't tie him in with the neat and clean-looking men who work in the bank my mother goes to. They wear suits and white shirts.

"Prison's no fun, lad."

"My father's in prison," I said. The words had popped out of my mouth before I could stop them. It was the first time I had ever said them out loud to anyone, though I had said them often enough inside my head.

He turned his head to look me in the face.

"I thought there was something up with you."

"He stole money, too. He embezzled it. He worked as a wages clerk."

"Aye, money's a temptation when you see it under your nose."

"I don't think it was that. He'd got into debt, bad debt. He was extravagant. He didn't cut his coat according to his cloth."

I told Rupert then about Aunt Janet and he thought she sounded like a nasty bit of work. I went on to tell him a great many other things, about my mother needing an operation, and how worried I was about her, and about the twins, and my friends Pete and Billy and Mike.

I was amazed at how much I told him. He sat and nodded.

"Travelling's better than all that, lad. Couldn't be bothered with folk wanting this and that of me."

When I'd finished talking I felt exhausted. A yawn like a tidal wave washed over me this time.

"I could be doing with a kip myself," said Rupert.

I lay back against the grass and let my eyes close. The last thoughts that came into my mind before I fell asleep were to do with my father. Would he take to the hills like a daft thing when he came out of prison? In ten years' time would he look like Rupert?

When I wakened I knew I had been asleep for a long time. And I still felt sleepy. I yawned and stretched and was tempted to drift off again but I struggled up and shook my head to try and clear it. The sun had changed, it had that soft, more buttery-yellow look of evening. My watch said seven.

And then I remembered Rupert. He had gone. I got up and looked around, peered up the road and across the fields but there was no sign of him. Had he ever been there? Or had I been dreaming?

"Did you see him, Gully? Or were you sleeping too?"

"Bikes need to kip as well, you know."

Gulliver looked strange. I hadn't had time yet to get used to his new colour. Everything was looking strange to me. Wakening up under the bridge after a long sleep had confused me.

I bent to pick up the bottle from the grass and when I

saw that the juice had been half drunk I knew that Rupert had been real. That he had sat here on the grass beside me. And had drunk from the bottle and told me about his life. And I had told him about mine.

"I suppose he doesn't like to stay in the same place too long, Gully. We'll need to get moving, too."

But first I must eat. I would have the cheese roll and an apple.

The strap of the food panier was undone. I frowned. I was sure I had fastened it.

"Didn't I, Gully?"

"I saw you do it."

I pulled open the bag. The cheese roll was not there. And a packet of dates had gone. *And* a bar of chocolate. *And* a packet of nuts and raisins. *And* an apple, and a banana. I couldn't believe it. I had so been looking forward to that cheese roll. I rummaged right to the bottom of the panier but there was no doubt about it — most of my food had been stolen! And I didn't have to think very hard to know who had done it.

"What a nerve, Gully!"

"And after you gave him the ham roll!"

I ran up the embankment and scanned the fields again in case Rupert should be lurking about, in a ditch or under a hedge.

"Thief!" I shouted. "Once a thief always a thief!"

6

All the Fun of the Fair

The road into Perth was busy with traffic that evening. A car passed us every minute. It was Saturday, I remembered.

Coming into the city from the south, there's a huge park with a road cutting through it. As I cycled up the road, I saw ahead the reason why there were so many cars about.

"There's a fair on, Gully!"

I cycled faster. Although it wasn't dark yet the lights of the fairground sparkled. I heard music. And I saw the big wheel turning against the sky. Looking behind, I put out my right hand and when the road was clear, crossed over to the park.

I got off Gulliver and pushed him round the back of the parked caravans and trucks into the middle of the fair. The place was seething with people. Everyone in Perth must have been there! It was difficult to manoeuvre Gulliver in and out of the crowd but I couldn't possibly have left him anywhere. I could have made him pretty safe but what was I to do with the paniers, and the sleeping bag? I was already carrying the rucksack on my back.

"Watch where you're going!" A woman, who had a small child by each hand, gave me a dirty look, even though I hadn't been anywhere near them. I tried to keep as much out of the way as possible. For a while I stood at the side of the coconut shy watching. Most people seemed to be in a good mood. They laughed when they scored and they laughed when they missed.

"Want a shot?" asked the man.

I shook my head and moved on. I couldn't afford to spend money on fairs, though I might treat myself later to some candy floss or an iced lolly or a poke of chips. I couldn't decide which.

Small children rode on a roundabout, clutching the ears of horses and giraffes and elephants. I wondered what the twins were doing and for a moment felt really funny inside. The thing that I was feeling might have been what was called homesickness. But if it were it seemed odd that I should be suffering from it in the middle of all these people having a good time when I hadn't felt it sitting alone under the old railway bridge.

I gave myself a shake and moved on again, to the big wheel. It soared high up into the sky and when it turned at the top and swooped down all the passengers shrieked as if they thought they were going to topple right out. On Pete's birthday his dad took us to the fair at Portobello, outside Edinburgh, and we'd had a ride on the wheel. I wished Pete was there now.

"Don't be such a twit," said Gulliver. "You'd think you were a baby! Anyway, you've got me, haven't you?"

"Sorry, Gully!"

"Fancy a shot on the wheel?" asked someone beside me.

I turned and saw a fat lady, a very fat lady, not just fat in the way that some of my mother's friends think they are. (They're always talking about going on diets.) She was ginormous and I wondered for a moment if she worked at the fair. But it seemed not for she was wearing a going-out sort of dress with red poppies on it and she had a handbag slung over her shoulder.

"It looks good fun, doesn't it?" she said.

I nodded.

"Come on, I'll treat you!" I must have looked startled for she added, "It's all right, there's nothing to *worry* about."

"I'm not worried," I said, though I was a little. But there were plenty of people around, after all. Thousands of them. "It's just that I can't lay my bike down or my stuff might get pinched."

"We could put it in the back of my car. Have you got a chain for your bike?"

"Well, yes, but —"

"You'd like to go on the big wheel, wouldn't you?"

I looked up at it again.

"Yes," I said.

"Come on, then."

She led the way and I followed. I was feeling embarassed now and didn't know how to get out of it. She kept turning to talk to me. She told me that she'd been dying to have a ride on the wheel all evening but didn't like to go on her own. So she was going to come on it with me!

She stopped beside a Mini in the car park.

"This is my steed," she said.

It looked a very small car for such a big lady. She opened up the back and I stowed my luggage away, then we chained Gulliver to the back bumper.

"It won't be for long, Gully," I told him inside my head.

"It had better not be! Do you think I'm going to enjoy being chained to the back of this silly wee car?" He's a terrible snob, is Gulliver. Now if the car had been a Jaguar or a Ferrari he probably wouldn't have complained. "Not a snob," he objected. "I just like things that are more interesting. But a Mini!" He sounded disgusted.

"Shall we go?" said the Mini's owner. "Your bike'll be all right there."

Gulliver snorted. I turned my back on him and walked off with the woman. As we came under the lights I saw that her eyes were shining. Just before we reached the big wheel she told me that her name was Poppy.

I looked at the poppies on her dress.

"They're my favourite flower. Not surprising, eh? And what do they call you?"

"Mungo," I said, before I'd thought, and could have bitten my tongue out. But there was no time to start going on at myself for the wheel was stopping and the people were getting out. Poppy surged forward and grabbed us a chair.

It wasn't easy getting fitted into it. Poppy laughed.

"I'll hold my breath, Mungo, and you squeeze in."

I managed it but I felt like a sardine squashed right up against the edge. Poppy gripped the bar in front.

"Hold on then, Mungo! Here we go!"

Slowly we began to rise and the ground fell away below us. I looked down at the people on the ground who watched us with upturned faces.

"Isn't this marvellous? cried Poppy and gave another laugh, one that sounded big enough to float right over the top of the whole fairground.

I nodded.

"You're a very quiet boy."

I felt a bit of a killjoy so I said, "It's great."

We were at the top of the wheel's flight now and for a second seemed to hover on the brink. I gazed down on the world. It looked quite still, almost like a photograph. I felt one of Poppy's hands-clutching mine. And then before we could catch another breath we went rushing downwards, down, down, down, through the night air, and the faces and lights below came nearer, and I screamed too with everyone else. It *was* great.

We climbed up again. And swooshed down again. Up and down, up and down we went, and nothing else mattered but the going up and the coming down.

Now, far too soon, the wheel was beginning to turn more slowly. We came to rest with a slight bump.

Poppy took a paper hanky from her bag and wiped the tears from her eyes. I helped her climb out of the chair and get back down on to the ground.

"Thank you very much," I said. "That was fantastic."

"We're not done yet! What about the dodgems, Mungo? Are you game?"

"Sure!"

We chose a red car.

"You can drive," she said.

So I climbed in and took the wheel.

"Kid on you're Jackie Stewart."

"My dad says — " I began and stopped.

"What does your dad say?"

"That Jackie Stewart's the best racing driver there ever was," I finished up limply.

"Does your dad drive?"

"No. We don't have a car."

"Does he ride a bicycle?"

Fortunately, the power came on before she could ask any more questions and the cars started to move. I did what she had suggested and she egged me on. "That's it, Jackie, give it all you've got!" I spun the wheel, I dodged and I bumped, and when anyone came after us Poppy screamed and covered her eyes with her hands. My father would have said she knew how to enjoy herself.

She had to use another paper hanky when the session ended.

"That was marvellous, Mungo. You're going to be a brilliant driver when you're older."

I decided she wasn't half bad after all. In fact, it was a pity I couldn't have had her for an aunt instead of my mother's sister.

Aunt Janet would probably be ringing the police station every ten minutes. "Are you sure he hasn't been sighted, Sergeant? I can't understand how you haven't found him yet. You've had all day."

I smiled to myself. I was feeling quite pleased with the

38

way I'd managed to lie low for the day and now that I was in the middle of the fair I felt quite safe. Being with Poppy made me even safer, I realised, for the police would be looking for a boy on his own.

"What would you like to do now, Mungo? Shall we have some candy floss?"

While we ate it we strolled around.

"Do you live in Perth, Mungo?"

"I've got friends here."

That seemed to satisfy Poppy, at least for the moment. She didn't seem a very curious sort of person. Some people aren't, I've found, they just take you as you come.

We came to the Hall of Mirrors. We went in.

"Look, Mungo, look!" cried Poppy, pointing at herself in the mirror.

She was so skinny and stretched out that the poppies had almost turned into long red lines. And I was like a ten foot high stick insect! We couldn't help laughing.

"That's what I'd like to look like, Mungo."

I preferred her large, though not as large as she was in the next mirror. Even I had rolls of fat in that one. I looked like a Michelin boy.

"It's crazy," said Poppy, her eyes streaming. "Crazy!"

The next mirror made us short and wide so that our necks disappeared and our heads were all squashed-looking. We laughed so much we got stitches in our sides.

We went round all the mirrors twice and then I had to dash outside. I couldn't take any more. I gulped the air and rubbed my stomach. My jaw was aching, too. But I felt pretty good.

Poppy came rolling out, busy with the paper tissues. She shook her head, she could hardly speak.

"Let's have an iced lolly," she said when she did.

We had two each — such extravagance! — to quench our thirst, then we went on the ghost train which made Poppy shriek some more and clutch me and after that we had a go at the coconut shy.

I won a doll in a pink dress. I gave it to Poppy and she hugged it to her very large bosom. We tried everything in the fair, except the small kids' things like the roundabout that were too young for us.

The crowd was thinning out, some of the fair people were packing up.

"Last ride on the wheel," called the man in charge.

"Let's have a last ride," said Poppy.

It was dark now. The lights looked brighter than they had earlier before the sun had gone down. It must be quite late, I thought, as we soared up, up, up, towards the stars, but it didn't matter to me, nor to Poppy either it seemed.

When the wheel came down to the ground for the last time we sat for a moment not moving.

Poppy sighed. "Ah well, all good things come to an end."

I didn't like the sound of that.

7

Betrayal

"Will your friends not be worrying about you?" asked Poppy.

"They're not expecting me until tomorrow." I was glad that it was dark and she couldn't see my face. It must have been the colour of a ripe tomato. "I set off a day early."

"So what are you going to do now?"

"I thought I'd camp. It's a warm night."

"You could come home with me. I've got a spare bed lying there doing nothing."

"Oh, no, I couldn't do that," I said quickly.

"Why not? Wouldn't your mum like it?"

"No," I said, thankful that she had given me the excuse. And my mum *wouldn't* have liked it. She'd warned me never ever to go home with strangers, no matter how nice they seemed. And Poppy *was* nice. But she seemed to understand.

"That's okay," she said and stood up. My left leg had gone to sleep from having been squashed up against the side of the chair. I had to give it a good rub to get rid of the terrible prickle of pins and needles.

We walked back to the car. Gulliver was still there and showed no signs of having been bumped or scratched. I'd been worried about that whenever I'd thought about it.

"You didn't think about it too often though, did you?" he said, when I bent over him to take the chain off. "You were too busy enjoying yourself."

Poppy had opened up the back of the Mini. She wasn't as jolly as she'd been in the fairground, she was frowning a bit. I supposed she didn't want me to go. I lifted out the two paniers and my sleeping bag and strapped them on to Gulliver. Then I hoisted my rucksack up on to my back. I didn't feel one bit like cycling on through the night. But I would have to, for I didn't dare camp in Perth and risk a policeman tripping over me.

"Are you hungry, Mungo?" asked Poppy. "Would you fancy a fish supper? I know a café that's open late."

I was very hungry and at the thought of fish and chips my mouth watered.

"Come on! I'll go ahead and drive slowly and you can follow me." I was glad she hadn't asked me to get *in* the car for I'd definitely have said no to that!

She drove out of the park into the streets of the town. It was easy to follow, there was so little traffic about.

"I hope you know what you're doing," said Gulliver.

"Don't be silly! She's harmless."

"Remember Rupert! You thought he was okay too, didn't you? You trusted him."

"Well, not really. I don't know what else I could have done about him. But Poppy's not going to steal from me. She's not at all like Rupert. She's got money and a car and a house. And we're not going to go *to* her house."

We passed two policemen on foot and my mouth went dry but the Mini didn't stop. It pulled up outside a café.

"Do you want to put your stuff back in the car?" asked Poppy.

But I decided I might just as well leave it where it was. I could park Gulliver right outside the window and keep an eye on him.

We went in and took the table in front of the window. There were only two other people in the café, a man and woman who were eating chicken and chips. The smell of food made me realise how hungry I actually was. I'd not had much to eat that day. After I'd wakened to find that Rupert had flown I'd eaten a bag of nuts and raisins, an orange and a banana, but that wasn't enough to keep body and soul together, as my mother would say. The thought of her went through me like a knife.

"Are you all right?" asked Poppy.

"Fine." Just remember Aunt Janet! I told myself. That was all I had to do to know that there was no turning back.

Poppy went to the counter to order our fish suppers and brought back two steaming cups of tea for us to be getting on with.

"This is nice," she said. She smiled across the table at me. "I'd have liked to have had children of my own, you know. Then I'd always have had someone to go to the fair with, wouldn't I?"

"You're not married?"

"I almost was once. He got knocked down by a truck. He died next day."

I didn't know what to say. Poppy sighed and her whole body moved, and the poppies on her dress rippled.

"Have you any brothers or sisters, Mungo?"

"Two sisters. They're twins."

"That must be nice."

"For them maybe. Not for me." Poppy looked surprised so I added, "They're a lot younger than me. And they're not interested in anything *I* do."

"I bet you've got a nice mum, though. And what about your dad?"

"He's dead."

"I thought you said —"

"He died in May."

"I'm sorry about that."

I shrugged.

Poppy pushed back her chair and got up. "I'm just going to the Ladies for a minute, Mungo. Our fish'll not be long."

Off she went. I looked through the window and checked on Gulliver who made a face at me and then I looked back at the café. I saw the sign TOILETS written up on the wall and an arrow pointing in the direction one should go, and under the sign was another saying TELEPHONE. *Telephone*? My heart just about dropped into my stomach. She couldn't be — !

I got up and followed the arrow which took me up a passage at the side of the café. At the end of it was a brown door. Very carefully, I eased it open. I heard Poppy's voice. She was keeping it down but even so I could hear every word.

"You know that boy from Edinburgh who's run away? His name's Mungo McKinnon. I heard it on the radio."

44

I almost fell through the door into the passage on the other side. She *knew* who I was! And had known all along.

"Well, you see, Officer, I met him at the fair and now he's with me here at the White Owl café. I'm just going to give him a nice fish supper so don't come round for about twenty minutes. I want him to have time to enjoy it. Poor wee soul, he's starving."

The poor wee soul was fuming on the other side of the door. I had trusted her and she had betrayed me! In byegone days traitors had been drawn and quartered and hung from the town gates. I wanted to shout "Traitor!" at her through the crack in the door.

I shut the door and skedaddled as fast as I could back up the passage and into the café. I picked up my rucksack and made for the door.

"Your fish suppers are ready," the man behind the counter called after me, but I wasn't hungry any more though I knew I would be later.

I unchained Gulliver.

"You should have listened to me," he said.

"Shut your mouth!"

I leapt on to the saddle and before pedalling off glanced back through the café window. I saw Poppy's big moon-like face staring out at me. It looked startled. And sad.

But I had no time to think any more about Poppy just then, I had to get away before the police came. Where, though, should we go?

"Find somewhere to lie low," suggested Gulliver. "They'll catch us if we stay on the streets."

He was right. We went down one street and along another and then half way along the next I saw an open gate leading into a warehouse yard. I zoomed straight inside. The warehouse looked deserted though you can never quite tell with warehouses. I pushed the gate shut and put a brick behind it. And then took a very long deep breath.

"That was a close shave, Gully. We'll stick together in future, just the two of us."

"Now you're talking sense!"

What an idiot I'd been! And all the time I'd been thinking how *smart* I was. You see, I'd thought Poppy was a simple sort of woman, a bit thick in the head. I'd thought she wouldn't be suspicious about a boy of my age being out on his own at the fair. Even though I'd been pushing a bicycle loaded with things like sleeping bags and food! I needed to have my head examined.

So she'd recognised me from a radio report. But that didn't mean she had to hand me over to the police. Why couldn't she just have let me go on? I suppose she thought she was doing the 'right' thing.

"Car coming," said Gulliver.

I put my eye to a slit in the gate. It was a police car and it was cruising. After it had moved out of my sight I listened to the sound of its engine until, at last, it died away.

I put my sleeping bag on the ground and sat on it and ate nuts and dates and thought about fish and chips.

Whenever we heard a car I jumped up and watched it go by. I saw the police car one more time but it didn't stop. With a bit of luck the police might search for me on the road to Edinburgh thinking I was making for home. And right then, sitting in the cold junky yard, I wished I were at home in my nice warm bed.

"Don't be such a softie, Mungo McKinnon!" said Gulliver. "I never have a nice warm bed, do I?"

We squatted in the yard for about an hour and then I decided it might be safe to come out. I didn't want to stay there all night. I wanted to be well clear of Perth before morning.

Opening the gate, I peered out into the street. It was deserted, and dark between the pools of yellow which the street lights cast. I shivered even though it was not cold and wished again that I were in a warm bed and didn't have to set out on a night ride.

But quickly, before Gulliver could tick me off and before I would waste any more time wishing for things that could not be — such as, that my mother *didn't* have to go into hospital to have an operation or that my father *hadn't* had to go to prison — I wheeled Gulliver out and took off.

At the end of the street, I halted to look to left and right.

"Which way do you think, Gully?"

We had to get on to the A9 going north and I had no idea how to find it.

8

A Night Ride

For half an hour we went round in circles getting nowhere.

The same streets kept showing up again. It was like being trapped inside a maze. Perth is not all that big a town, not compared with a city like Edinburgh, but if you don't know your way about it can seem big enough. Especially at night when you can't see far ahead of you. And when you're worried about meeting police cars, or even Minis, at every intersection.

"It looks like we're lost, Gully."

"You can't give up like that."

"I'm not *giving* up!"

There was no moon, and no stars either. The sky had clouded over since we'd left the fairground. A shower of rain would be all that I needed!

"Stop being so miserable," said Gulliver. "Use your loaf!"

I stopped on a corner which was becoming only too familiar to try to think things out. If I could get to the river I should be able to find my way from there. On the opposite side of the Tay the ground rises upward and on that slope there are streets and houses. I climbed up on to a wall and looked about. There seemed to be lights on a higher level in one direction though I could not be certain. But I decided to make for it anyway. I had to do something.

My guess turned out to be right. As we neared the river I saw some road signs. I was so relieved that I let out a small cheer.

"For a while there, Gully, I thought we were done for."

"Never say die!"

That was one of my father's sayings. He used to say it when things looked black, when we were short of money or the chip pan caught fire and burnt out half the kitchen. One minute my mum would be crying and the next minute he'd have her laughing.

Would he be saying that now as he lay on his bed in his cell? He wouldn't be laughing, that was for sure. Or would he? He said you couldn't let things get you down. But he wasn't thinking about being locked up for years when he said it.

"Come on," said Gulliver, "give over! What's it to you what he's doing right now?"

"You're right, Gully. Let's get a move on."

We could travel at speed now. We soon left the town behind and were on the main road north.

I had been looking forward to that but had not bargained for the darkness. It was pitch black on the road except for the little circle of light the front lamp sent out ahead. But the circle was very little and the blackness huge all around us. It was one o'clock. It would be another three hours or so before the sky began to lighten again.

49

"We've got to keep going, Gully."

"What do you think I'm doing, Mutt Face?"

Just then Gulliver hit something, a stone maybe, and if it weren't for the fact that I was involved I would have said it served him right. He swerved, and in the next instant I was being catapulted over the top of the handlebars. I hit the road with a smack. The light went out.

I lay where I'd gone down getting my breath back. I heard one of Gulliver's wheels whirring. Then it stopped.

"Are you all right, Gully?"

There was no answer.

I'd have to get up and see but I didn't want to move. I felt as if I could have lain there for ever and perhaps I might have done if I hadn't seen the long streak of light up ahead. A car was coming towards us.

Rolling first on to my side, I got up on my knees. One of them hurt. The light was coming closer. Get a move on! I told myself and with a heave pushed up and was on my feet. Groping around, I found Gulliver and dragged him across to the edge of the road. We went stumbling over some rough ground and crashed into what turned out to be a wood.

As we collapsed, the car swept past, lighting up the road but not reaching as far as us. Soon afterwards it was followed by another and for a few moments I could see the curve of the road and the line that the trees made on the other side against the sky. Then the car was gone and it was dark and silent again. It seemed even darker than before.

I had never, as far back as I could remember, been

afraid of the dark. I was afraid of it now. I was scared. Dead scared. My whole body was shaking in a horrible way and I couldn't seem to stop it.

An owl hooted. Or something that sounded like an owl. But it didn't make me feel any better. All of a sudden I was aware of thousands of different sounds, croakings and cracklings and rustlings and goodness knows what else. The wood behind me was a big black cavern full of monsters.

"Stop it, Mungo McKinnon," said Gulliver, finding his tongue again. "Stop it!"

I had to take a hold of myself, as Aunt Janet would say. The thought of her steadied me a little.

"Silly Aunt Janet!" I shouted.

"Busybody Aunt Janet," said Gulliver.

In the letter to my mum I had said, "I know Aunt Janet hates me. I heard her say she didn't want to have me to stay but she knew where her duty lay. Well, I *hate* her too."

"Horrible Aunt Janet!"

Did someone laugh? Or was it just the wind in the trees?

I gripped my hands in front of me and held on tightly until the shaking stopped.

"Now go and find the lamp," said Gulliver, "and see if it's broken or not. Then we can see if we're broken, ha, ha!"

If the lamp *was* broken we wouldn't be able to go on until daylight. But if we couldn't go on how could we stay here in this terrible, unfriendly place? For that's what it felt like — downright unfriendly, as though it was full of creatures that wished us harm.

Gulliver was lying right beside me so it was easy enough to put my hand on the lamp. I tried to move the lever that should switch it on. It wouldn't move. It was stuck. And so were we!

"Find the torch, then," said Gulliver. "Don't just sit there!"

I fumbled around in the rucksack and pulled it out. Fortunately, it was still working. I checked Gulliver over. He wasn't badly hurt and had only a few scratches on his paintwork.

"That doesn't matter, does it, since you're going to be painting me again?"

I had only a scratch or two myself. My left knee was grazed and oozing blood. I cleaned it with tissues. I was beginning to feel better.

Hugging my knees up close to my chin, I considered our next move. To go out on the dark road without a light would be asking for trouble. "Never ever do that," my father had said. "All right," I said back to him, "I can think for myself!" If I went on to the road without a light I wouldn't even be able to see it.

I unrolled my sleeping bag and crawled right in so that only a small funnel was left for air. The monsters wouldn't be able to get at me now!

I dozed and wakened when dawn was breaking.

I had been dreaming and in my dream had been lying on the ground, pinned to it with thousands of tiny cords;

and advancing up my body, moving from the feet towards the trunk, were hundreds of midgets armed with tiny bows and arrows. For a moment after waking I thought I couldn't move. I lifted my head. I half expected to see the Emperor of Lilliput walking up my arm.

Instead, I saw my Gulliver sprawled on the dew-covered ground and beyond him the hazy shapes of trees whose crowns rose into the morning mist and whose lower branches interlocked, forming a thick, dense screen. But I no longer felt afraid of the wood. Not now that I could see it, though I wouldn't have wanted to go right into the still-dark heart of it.

I heard a rustle and a crackle somewhere behind us.

"Probably just a mouse or a vole, Gully."

"We're not afraid of mice or voles."

"Of course we're not!"

The mist was clearing very rapidly, the tops of the trees were showing and light was filtering in between the trunks. They were pine trees and smelt tangy and sweet. But I had no time to sit sniffing tree smells. I should be out on the road for at eight o'clock I must leave it again and find another hiding place.

I got to my feet and picked Gulliver up, brushing soil and pine needles from his saddle and straightening him out. Then I retied the load and heaved the rucksack up on to my back. The sky was all rosy pink and pale green. Ahead of us lay the road north.

9

The Abandoned House

Even though I was tired, I enjoyed that early morning ride. In the beginning, the sky was streaked with lots of soft colours; then it settled down to being a clear blue with little wispy bits of white trailing across it here and there. Traffic was light. For the first hour nothing at all passed us. It was Sunday morning. I felt as if I were the only person moving in the whole wide world. And the world seemed very wide, stretching far away on either side of us.

As we went further north the hills began to appear. Blue hills with craggy tops. The sight of them made me want to sing, except that I needed all my puff for cycling. The road dipped and rose. I moved the gears up and down.

"Ataboy, Gully, you're going great!"

I rang his bell and a horse grazing near the fence lifted his head to look at us. Horses, cows, sheep — they were all fine. Far better than cars and people. When a car did pass I turned my head to the side so that the driver wouldn't be able to see my face.

We didn't go through any towns or villages. The road passes them all by. When I'd come this way with my father we had turned off and gone into the villages — my father said you got a better feel of how the country

54

really was that way — but I couldn't afford to do that today.

Since I had decided that I must get off the road by eight, I was keeping a close watch on the time. Between half-past seven and eight I would turn off on to a side road and start looking for a good hiding place.

Half-past seven came and went and for a while after that there were no turnings off. More cars zipped past. I was getting jittery, expecting every time I heard one behind me that as it drew level it would turn out to be a police car. Then it would pull up in front and two policemen would get out, one from either side, and would come walking slowly towards me, their hands resting on their guns.

"Are you Mungo James McKinnon?"

"Stop letting your imagination run away with you!" said Gulliver. "You know very well the police don't carry guns here, unless it's for something unusual. And you're not unusual enough, Mungo McKinnon. You've been watching too much telly!"

Aunt Janet had once told me that I had too much imagination. I had been re-telling a story I'd heard at school about the great Scottish hero William Wallace and putting in quite a few gory details that she didn't care for.

"Don't be so bloodthirsty, Mungo," she said. And then, "You've got too much imagination, that's your trouble." She likes to tell people what their trouble is.

"There's no such thing as having *too* much imagination," said my father.

"How can you say that?" demanded Aunt Janet. "Sometimes it can amount to downright lying."

"I wasn't lying," I objected. "They did hack one another to death."

My mother had stepped in then to say tea was ready.

"There's a turning!" cried Gulliver. "You're not paying attention!"

I had almost missed it. If I had, that would have been Aunt Janet's fault too. She had a lot to answer for, that woman. I squeezed on the brakes, reversed Gulliver who was still grumbling, and escaped down the side road.

It was five past eight. I must not dither about. We passed a farm but there would be people about there. We came to a wood but it was small and thin and wouldn't give enough cover. We came to a humped-back bridge but a burn in full spate flowed beneath it.

"Don't panic," said Gulliver. "Just keep your eyeballs peeled!"

At half-past eight we still hadn't found anywhere that was right. We might have lain at the back of a wall for an hour or two, or gone behind some trees, but I was looking for a place to spend the day in. A place where I could relax and sleep for a few hours without worrying about someone stumbling over us.

And then I saw the house. It was large, with towers and turrets, and it stood in the middle of a piece of parkland. You could tell just by looking that no one was living there. The stone wall round the park was crumbling away, the gates were rusty and padlocked, and the drive overgrown with weeds.

"This should do us, Gully."

I picked him up and put him on the other side of the wall. Then I scrambled over myself.

"Not bad, eh?" I gazed around at the big copper beeches and the larches and the silver birches. And behind the house stretched a line of hills blue and purple and fir green.

"Get a move on!" said Gulliver. "You haven't time to stand and stare."

He was right. I jumped on and rode him up the bumpy rutted drive. As we got closer to the house my heart beat faster. What if there was someone living in there after all? But no, there couldn't be, the windows had a blank look even though there were curtains at the sides of them. And the curtains were old and dirty.

I went round the back. Weeds grew high, choking the yard, and tall, nasty-looking nettles stood on guard beside the back door. I tried the handle. It wouldn't budge. I would have to break in. Then I'd be a house-breaker and if I got caught I could be charged and sent to prison. Maybe not prison proper but those special schools they send delinquents to.

"If you don't watch him he'll end up as a delinquent," I'd overheard Aunt Janet say to my mother. "He's always been a bit on the wild side. And now that his father has set him such a bad example . . . ."

"For goodness sake!" said Gulliver. "You're not going to start paying attention to what *she* says, are you? You've got to get inside the house. We need shelter."

I made a tour of the downstairs windows. They were

all locked. I picked a small one and found a heavy stone. It was easy enough to crack a pane but less easy to pick the pieces of glass out of the frame. I managed to cut my thumb and had to get the plasters out of the rucksack.

"At this rate," said Gulliver, "you'll have none of those things left soon. Clumsy clot!"

It was just as well I was working at the back of the house, out of sight of the road. I had quite a bit of blood on my hands and tee-shirt by the time I got all the glass out. I peered into a pantry. With a heave I was up on the sill and going through.

Pots and pans lay on the shelves covered in dust. The sink was old-fashioned, very deep, and made of porcelain which was splotched with stains of many colours. No one had worked here for a long time.

I went through to the next room. This was a large kitchen, again old-fashioned, with a stone-flagged floor and a big black range for cooking, though there was also a manky-looking gas cooker. Cupboards lined the walls from floor to ceiling. Inside was crockery, heaps and heaps of it, and tinned food! It looked as if my luck was in.

Now to get Gulliver inside. He wouldn't be able to come through the broken window so I'd have to find a door that would open. The back door was locked, as I already knew, and there was no sign of a key. I hunted all over the kitchen and found a number of rusty keys but none that fitted.

Opening the kitchen door, I found myself in a dark passage. I groped my way along the wall looking for a light switch but when I found one and switched it on nothing happened. The elctricity must be turned off. I stood still to let my eyes adjust then I made my way into the middle of the house. A musty smell filled it. I supposed this was how a house would smell if it had been shut up for a while. The passage led to a wide hall from which a staircase ran upwards branching in two directions to meet again on the top landing. Once upon a time children might have run up and down these stairs laughing but it was difficult to imagine.

Gulliver would be thinking I'd forgotten him. I made for the front door.

It was locked and bolted but when I'd pushed back the two sets of bolts and turned the handle, it creaked open. I peered out. The coast seemed clear so I ran round the back and grabbed Gulliver.

I wheeled him into the house and closed the heavy door behind us. After the brightness outside, I could hardly see again.

Then there came a noise from overhead. A strange, unearthly noise.

"Don't tell me you've brought me into a haunted house," said Gulliver.

10

Bats in the Belfry

The noise came again, a flapping, shuffling sound. Goose pimples had sprung out all over the tops of my arms like tiny little mushrooms. I rubbed them to get the blood flowing.

"It's cold," I said.

"You're just scared," said Gulliver. "Cowardy cowardy custard!"

I had been about to say maybe we'd better go, that I didn't think I was going to like this house very much, but now I stood my ground.

"I dare you to go up and have a look," said Gulliver.

I had never been known to refuse a dare, not even when Billy had bet me that I hadn't the nerve to swim in the Water of Leith in February. There had been snow on the ground. My hair had frozen on the way home and my teeth clattered so hard against one another that they sounded like a tattoo. My mother hadn't thought it was funny. She told me I was a lunatic and that I would get pneumonia, but I didn't.

"Okay," I said to Gulliver, "I'll go and take a look. I'm sure there won't be anything there, anyway."

I left him in the bottom hall and went marching up the stairs whistling the tune from the *The Bridge on the River Kwai*. On the staircase wall there were pictures of men

60

and women who looked like ancestors. Sombody's ancestors. Whose, I wondered? And *had* they left a ghost behind them?

The top landing was quite sunny and bright, compared to the hall below. The house felt better up here. And then I heard the noise again. I stopped and listened. It was coming from the floor above.

I didn't march now, or whistle. I crept along the landing, past the closed doors, until I came to a staircase leading upwards. It was much narrower than the main one and it twisted out of sight. I was getting warmer. The noise was growing louder.

I paused with my foot on the bottom stair. Did I really want to go on with this? I didn't have to. But I did want to find out what was making such a strange noise. Curiosity killed the cat, Aunt Janet is always telling the twins, who like to poke in her bag when she comes. But she's softer with them than with me even when she's telling them off and she'll bring something for them out of her bag. "You're too big a boy to need presents," she says to me, but I wouldn't take anything from her if she paid me. At Christmas and birthdays she gives me pyjamas, vests or socks.

Gulliver would be getting restless down below. I put my foot on the second stair. It creaked. I had known it would before I trod on it. They were those kind of stairs. The whole house seemed to be creaking and groaning like an old, tired man.

Up I went, round and round, putting my hand against the wall to steady myself. I might not be all that old but I was certainly tired. I had to watch my step or I might easily have slipped. My head was beginning to feel giddy, the way it had after I broke my ankle playing football.

A door faced me at the top of the stairs. The noise was coming from behind it. I hesitated, let one foot slide back to the step below. "Custard," chanted Gulliver down in the hall. "Cowardy, cowardy . . ." I reached out and took hold of the handle.

As the door opened something came whirling out and skimmed right over the top of my head. The shock sent me reeling backwards against the wall. I let out a shriek, I couldn't help it. I went down on to my knees, clutching my head between my hands. The thing was battering itself against the wall. Peering between my fingers I saw that it was black. And that it was a bat.

I'd like to pretend that then I wasn't scared any more but I'd be lying if I did. I hate bats. I hate their funny little eyes and I hate the way they flap about. When this one turned back towards me I curled up and put my hands over my head to protect it. I knew that if bats get into your hair they can get stuck there. It happened to my father once. Wait until I told him about this! But of course I wouldn't be telling him anything.

The bat flew back inside the door and quickly I got up to close it behind him. Before I did I glanced into the room and what I saw made me feel sick. It was a turret and it seemed to be full of bats and birds. Perhaps there were no more than half a dozen but it looked like a multitude.

The air quivered with whirring wings. One bird was flailing itself against the window. I wanted to go and let it out but how could I cross the room? Looking down, I saw that the floor was littered with dead birds and skeletons of birds, some whole, some crumbling away. I pulled the door shut.

I stood on the top step, shaking. There must be an open or a broken window which was allowing the birds and bats to come in and once in, they couldn't find their way out. I felt I should help them but I was too exhausted to do anything but totter back down the stairs to Gulliver.

"What you need," he said, "is a good kip. Go find yourself a room."

Sometimes Gulliver talks sense.

I took my sleeping bag and hiked back up the stairs. My legs ached. I went along the landing in the opposite direction from the turret.

The first room I tried had a four-poster bed with scabby-looking curtains. I didn't fancy sleeping in that, I thought I might have nightmares.

The second room was a kind of sitting room with big buttoned leather chairs in dark red. Above the mantle-piece was a rack of pipes of all shapes and sizes. On a small table lay a long-stemmed one half-filled with mouldering tobacco looking as if it had been put down by someone who had meant to come back later but had never got round to it. I seemed to be in a smoking room. I'd seen one before in a telly play about a mystery in a country house. This was a country house and I suspected it might have a mystery too.

The third room was a children's room. There were

toys and books and two single beds. I flung my bag on top of one of the beds and crept inside.

This business of sleeping and waking at all the wrong times was really mixing me up. Each time I woke I didn't know where I was for the first few minutes.

I sat up and looked about. On the opposite wall were photographs of two girls in silver frames. They looked like twins but they weren't Susie and Cathy. They were older and they had long fair hair held back by bands on the top of their heads. Their eyes were blue, cornflower blue. They looked a bit like the pictures of Alice in Wonderland.

The room was papered in a pink, green and white flowery pattern, and the curtains were pink. Faded pink. The carpet looked faded too, especially in front of the window. In the corner was a rocking horse and a doll's house and an old gramophone like the one my granny used to have. When she died my father wanted to keep it but my mum said we hadn't enough room for all the stuff we had as it was.

The wall on the other side was covered with shelves. Some of them held books, on the rest sat dolls neatly arranged in rows. They stared back at me with glazed eyes. Why had the girls gone away and left all their toys?

It was terribly still and warm in the room. I sneezed. The dust lay thick, on everything.

I wriggled out of my sleeping bag and went over to the bookshelves. I picked out a book, *The Wind in the Willows*.

I'd read that myself, had it at home. My father had given it to me for my ninth birthday. Everything I touched or looked at reminded me of him. It wasn't fair!

I opened the book. There was an inscription on the fly leaf.

'Christmas 1953,' it said, in black, sloping writing. 'To Jane, with love from Mother and Father.'

The pages smelt musty when I pressed them to my face. Then I caught sight of another book on the shelves, one that I also had. In fact, I had it with me, in my rucksack. *Gulliver's Travels*! I took it down. The edition was identical to mine, and had the same cover, with Gulliver lying flat on his back fastened to the ground with thin cords and the little people of Lilliput crawling all over him.

Again, there was an inscription on the fly leaf.

'Christmas 1954,' it said, in the same handwriting. 'To Fanny, with love from Mother and Father.'

So the twins were called Fanny and Jane.

I went over to the gramophone. A record lay on the turntable. I gave it a wipe then put it back and wound up the machine.

'Daisy, daisy,' it played, 'give me your answer, do. I'm half crazy, all for the love of you . . .'

The sound was tinny and seemed to come from a long way off, not from the machine under my nose.

'. . . I can't afford a carriage, but you'll look sweet upon the seat of a bicycle built for two.'

That reminded me of my own bicycle built for one. I'd have to go downstairs and see that he was all right. I lifted the arm of the gramophone and the music stopped. Later, I might try some of the other records.

"You've been a long time," said Gulliver. "It's evening."

And I had eaten hardly anything all day. I checked out the food in the pantry but the tins looked ancient. I ate some dates and nuts and raisins and my last orange. Tomorrow I'd have to risk going to a shop.

I had the whole of the downstairs to explore but I didn't feel up to it just then. I wanted to go out. The walls, even though they were big, were making me feel restless, and the fusty smell made me want fresh air.

"We'll go for a spin, Gully. We'll go on a reccy to see if there's a village nearby."

Gulliver seemed pleased by that suggestion. He had probably had enough of leaning against the wall in the dark passage.

Outside smelt good. It smelt of evening, of warm grass and flowers. Dozens of wild flowers that I hadn't had time to notice earlier. They were growing all over the parkland and up the sides of the drive. Red and white clover, poppies, harebells, ladies slipper . . . . The scent of clover was very strong. I took a deep breath.

"Okay," said Gulliver, "but just keep moving. We don't want to be seen coming down the drive, do we?"

We got down the drive and over the wall without seeing anyone. We turned right and after cycling for about a mile I saw the roofs of a small grey stone village ahead. I slowed.

The village was very small, not much more than a hamlet. I hesitated on the edge of it, wondering whether I should ride on. But there seemed to be no one about. And it had only one street so I could whizz through that in no time.

The street was lined on either side with single-storeyed stone cottages. One, near the end of the row, was a shop, of the kind that would sell everything from matches to sausages, with a pillar box outside; and a few yards further on, there was a telephone box.

I cycled past the box, then turned and came back and stopped in front of it.

"I'm going to ring Pete, Gully."

"Watch what you say, then!"

"Of course I will!"

My hands shook as I dialled the number. At home they never shook. "Nerves," Aunt Janet would say. She was supposed to suffer from them herself and I was supposed to be kind to her because of that.

"Hello." I almost dropped the receiver when I heard a voice above the bleeps at the other end. It belonged to Mandy, Pete's sister. "Hello," she said again. I put the money in.

Trying to sound like somebody else, I asked for Pete.

"Just a minute," she said and I thought her voice had changed. Don't be silly, I told myself, you're far too jumpy.

Pete came then to the phone. "Hi," he said.

"Don't say anything, Pete," I said quickly, cutting off

his cry of surprise. "It's Mungo. Would you give my mum a message? Tell her I'm fine and she's not to worry."

"Where are you?"

"I can't tell you."

"Everybody's going crazy. Where *are* you?" he yelled.

Now I could hear voices behind his, Mandy's and his mother's. I put down the receiver.

"I could have told you it would be like stirring up a hornet's nest," said Gulliver.

I pedalled fast back to the house, wanting to get indoors again, out of sight. Out of everybody's sight.

The sun had slipped behind the hills. The air was calm and quiet and the smell of the clover seemed even stronger than before. I felt pleased that I had found this house even though it had mould in its kitchen and bats in its belfry.

"Tower," said Gulliver. He can be a real know-all at times.

I clambered in through the window and went into the hall to open the front door and bring Gulliver in. And then I stood still.

There was not much light left in the hall but there was enough for me to see, standing at the foot of the stairs, the figure of a girl in a light-coloured dress. She had her hand on the newel post. Then she turned and saw me and she, too, stood still.

I took a step closer and I saw her face. It was the same as the girls in the photographs upstairs.

11

Fanny

"How did you get in?" I asked and hoped my voice was steady for I had never met a ghost before. It was a pretty silly question, anyway, since I was sure she had been in the house all the time, that she *belonged* to it.

"Through the window."

"Not through the looking glass?"

She laughed. "I'm not Alice."

"Who are you then?"

"Fanny."

"I knew it! Well, that you were either Fanny or Jane."

"Really?" She took a step closer to me now. She might easily have stepped out of one of the picture frames on the bedroom wall. "How amazing!"

"You look just like your photograph."

"Do I?" It was too dark to make out the colour of her eyes, though I supposed they were blue, like the ones in the photograph, but I could see that they were very wide open. "Who are *you* then?"

"Mungo. Mungo McKinnon." I saw no reason to lie to a ghost.

"I don't think we've met." She held out her hand and I took it. It felt surprisingly warm. "I suppose you broke the window?"

"Well, yes. I had to. I needed somewhere to stay."

"Don't you have a home?"

"Not at the moment."

"Are you an orphan?"

"A half orphan. My father's dead."

"I'm sorry."

From overhead came the dreadful sounds made by the creatures in the turret.

"What's that?" cried Fanny, tilting her head back to look upward.

"The bats and birds in the turret. Didn't you know?"

"Why should I know?"

"It's your house, isn't it?"

"This is the first time I've ever been here."

"It can't be!"

"It is."

It had grown so dark that I could no longer see the look on her face.

"Let's go into the kitchen," I said. "I saw some candles on the shelf there."

She followed me though I kept glancing round in case she would disappear. The kitchen was lighter. I found the candles and also some matches. There were several large boxes.

"They look ancient," said Fanny, coming up beside me, and as she moved she brushed against my arm, making me tremble a little. "Do you think they'll strike?"

"Everything in this house is ancient." I struck the first match. It made a dull sound and remained dead. I tried another. The sticks felt soft between my fingers. "I have a torch upstairs," I said, then stopped. I frowned. I couldn't remember seeing it when I looked in my ruck-sack earlier. "Gosh, I think I may have left it in the wood!"

"What wood?"

"It's a long story."

"You are a strange boy."

I thought she was a fine one to be talking about being strange! I was still having no luck with the matches. Perhaps we were going to be doomed to darkness. "They're dead as dodos," I said.

"The house has been shut up for thirty years so it's not surprising."

"So you do know about it?"

"Of course. It belongs to my grandfather."

"Ah! Is he a ghost too?"

"A ghost?" She laughed. She pinched my arm. "Do I feel like a ghost?"

At that moment the match between my fingers hissed and burst into a small flame which I quickly held to the candle wick. It caught. I held up the light and looked into Fanny's face. She *did* look real enough. Her eyes were still laughing. And they were blue, cornflower blue.

"But I don't understand," I said.

"Neither do I," she said.

"Come upstairs!"

I led the way up to the bedroom where I had slept. I held the candle so that she could see the two photo-graphs.

"Have you ever seen these before?"

She shook her head.

"They're called Fanny and Jane."

"They're my aunts, then," she said.

So maybe we were getting somewhere at last. "It's funny, though, that you've never seen their photographs before."

"It is, isn't it? I asked Grandpa once if he had any photographs of them and he said he didn't. Though he has some of my father when he was a boy."

"Where are your aunts now?"

"Aunt Fanny lives in Australia. She married a sheep farmer. I've only seen her once."

"And Jane?"

"She's dead. She died when she was a child, I think. Nobody will talk about her. What time is it?" Fanny caught hold of my wrist and looked at my watch. "Goodness, I must go or Fyffie will be going mad! She's our housekeeper. Mrs Fyffe."

"Don't you have any parents?"

"They're in Peru most of the time. My father works there. So I'm a sort of grass orphan, as Fyffie calls me. You know — like a grass widow whose husband isn't dead but away a lot of the time?"

"Like my mother."

"I thought you said your father was dead?"

I didn't know what to say to that. I felt uncomfortable but Fanny let it pass and made a move towards the door. She thought Mrs Fyffe might send out a search party if she didn't come home soon.

"I should have been in an hour ago."

I lighted her way down the stairs. Our shadows

showed up on the walls, looking long and thin. I remembered standing in the Hall of Mirrors with Poppy and it seemed a long time ago. Time seemed to be doing funny things altogether.

"You might as well use the front door," I said.

I tugged it open. Fanny paused on the step.

"I'll come back and see you tomorrow, shall I?"

I nodded.

"Would you like some food?"

"Yes, please." I cleared my throat which seemed to have dried up. "You won't — well, tell anyone about me, will you?"

"No, of course not. You won't tell anyone about me either, will you?"

"No."

"Goodnight, Mungo."

"Goodnight, Fanny."

I watched her pale dress flit like a butterfly down the drive and go over the wall and vanish. Then I went to fetch Gulliver.

"You almost forgot about me, didn't you? Who was she, anyway?"

"I'm not sure," I said and wheeled him inside.

12

Curiouser and Curiouser

If I had been confused waking on other mornings, it was nothing compared to this one. I sat bolt upright staring at the photographs of Fanny and Jane and wondering whether I had been dreaming or talking to a ghost. Perhaps she was in the room now, watching me. Perhaps she was laughing at me. But no, I didn't think she'd do that. She'd *seemed* too nice for that.

My father had seen a ghost once, though my mother said she didn't believe it. And Aunt Janet said, of course, that he had too much imagination. He had been walking up a glen in the north of Scotland at dusk and had seen a figure — a woman — coming out of a ruined cottage. She had been dressed in a rough skirt and shawl. She vanished as my father came closer. The glen was one that had been cleared during the Highland Clearances, when crofters had been turned out of their homes so that their land could be rented to sheep farmers for more money. My father was convinced that she had been an evicted crofter.

I wished that he were here now so that I could talk to him about Fanny. Yes, I wished it, and the wish would not go away, even when I asked myself who would want to talk to a convict? I went downstairs and made do with Gulliver.

"She's different, Gully, from any other girl I know."

"You don't know all that many. There are the twins but they don't count, they're too young. And then there are the girls in your class at school."

But I didn't know many of them all that well. Sometimes we played chasey with them but most of the time in the playground we stuck together, Pete and Mike and Billy and I.

"Hello," said Fanny behind me and I nearly leapt out of my skin. "Who were you talking to just now? Another ghost?" And she laughed. She didn't look at all like one in daylight. Her cheeks were pink and her fair hair shone the way the twins' hair does when it's newly washed.

My face must have had that ripe tomato look again. And once more I didn't know what to say.

"I suppose if you're on your own a lot you end up talking to yourself?" she said.

"I suppose so."

"I've brought you something to eat." She had a basket over her arm. "I'm a bit like Little Red Riding Hood!"

"But I'm not a wolf."

We both laughed and went through to the kitchen where Fanny laid out the food. Brown bread — "Baked by Fyffie, her bread's delicious!" — and butter and a large lump of Orkney cheese and a piece of chicken, two tomatoes, a banana and a slab of apple pie. And there was orange juice to drink, and a flask of hot chocolate. And she had brought a new box of matches.

"How did you get all that out of the house?"

"I told Fyffie I was going for a picnic. She always makes huge picnics."

"Shall we save some for later and go for a real picnic?" I would have to get out of the house for a while, I wouldn't be able to stay shut up in it all day.

Fanny said she knew somewhere we could go, somewhere tucked away where no one would see us.

"I like secrets." She smiled.

I was starving, I realised. Fanny watched me eat. She had already eaten, she said, when I asked her.

"Fyffie always makes me eat what she calls a proper breakfast."

"Do you live on your own with her?"

"And my grandfather. That's in holiday time. In term time I go away to school, to England."

So she went to boarding school. She *was* quite different from anyone else I knew.

"I hate it," she said. "It's like being in prison."

I spilled my hot chocolate and had to mop it up.

"Why did you jump when I said 'prison'?" She noticed too many things, did Fanny.

I shrugged.

"Is it because you feel as if you're locked up when you're in here?"

"Maybe."

"I'd like to stay here in Perthshire all year round, with Fyffie and Grandpa. But my parents won't let me. They say I should be with girls of my own age. It's difficult getting to do what you want, isn't it? To be *free*. Though you seem to manage it?"

"Only for just now. It won't last for ever."

"No, I don't suppose it could."

She spoke very precisely and stopped every now and then to think what she wanted to say.

I finished my breakfast and we repacked the basket.

"Shall we go and take a look round the house first?" she suggested. "While it's broad daylight? I'm dying to see it."

"Why haven't you seen it before?"

"My grandfather keeps the place locked up. No one is allowed in."

"Why not?"

"He says it's unsafe."

"It doesn't seem unsafe to me."

"I think there may be some other reason," said Fanny "but I have no idea what it is," and led the way forward.

"Haven't you asked him?"

"Of course! But you can't make people talk if they don't want to, can you?"

"No," I agreed, "you can't."

The first room we looked into was the drawing room. It would have been very grand but for the dust sheets covering the furniture. Lifting the corners of the cloths, we saw velvet-covered sofas and chairs, small tables with curly legs and a grand piano. A chandelier hung from the centre of the ceiling, its pieces moving in the draught of air coming in from the open door.

Fanny played a few notes on the piano.

"It's got a nice tone, at least it would if it was tuned. I must ask Grandpa to bring it over to the house."

"But you can't, can you? Without telling him you've been here?"

"No, of course I can't. Pity." She closed the lid. "I wonder if Fanny and Jane played it."

I had a feeling that they did. The house gave me a lot of feelings like that. As we walked round it I felt as if other people were looking over our shoulders remembering things that had happened long ago.

We went into the other rooms, one by one: the dining room, a second, smaller sitting room, a library with glass-fronted bookcases stacked with leather-bound books, a study with a large desk and several cupboards, all locked.

"How annoying," said Fanny, tugging at the desk drawer. "We might have found out something interesting."

The furniture in all the rooms was draped in white except for the games room. The billiard table stood uncovered in the centre with two cues looking as if they had just been flung down, and several balls were scattered about.

"It looks like the people in the house left in a hurry," I said.

"Except that *somebody* came back to put on the dust sheets." Fanny picked up one of the cues. "Come on, let's have a go!"

I lifted the other cue. "You first!"

She crouched low over the baize and took aim. She hit the white cue ball and it went careening into a number of others raising a cloud of dust. It was my turn, then. I chalked my cue and lined up with the cue ball. I took my time. "Never hurry," my father said. I hit the ball and it struck the red I was aiming for. We watched it go rolling over the green baize. On the brink of the pocket it hovered then plopped down in. Fanny cheered.

"Who taught you to play?" she asked.

"My father." The words were out before I could pull them back.

"Mungo, how can your father be dead and yet not dead?"

"He's in jail."

"Goodness! How interesting."

Interesting was a word that Fanny liked. I said it was not at all interesting to have a father in prison.

"Is he a murderer?"

"Of course not!"

"I'm sorry. You're not angry, are you?"

I was a little, but said I wasn't. We put the cues back on the table and wiped the dust off our hands.

"What did he do, or don't you want to tell me?"

"He embezzled money. He got into debt. He was extravagant, you see. He didn't cut his coat according to his cloth."

"Sounds just like my Great-Uncle Jack. He was an embezzler, too, but his father paid the money and Jack was sent away to Africa to farm. You know, most families have a skeleton in their closet, that's what Fyffie says."

I didn't like my father being referred to as a skeleton in a closet though I didn't think Fanny meant to be nasty as Billy would have if he had said it. She was trying to comfort me, I thought. And at least she hadn't been shocked when she'd heard that my father was a jail bird.

"McKinnon's father is a jail bird," some of the boys had chanted in the playground at school.

I said to Fanny, "We don't have money like that in our family to pay off debts and things. We're poor." I had never thought so before but alongside Fanny's family, we seemed to be. "Not like people in Ethiopia or anything like that," I added quickly. "I mean they're *really* poor. We have enough to eat and a place to live in."

"Tell me more about your family!"

But I had had enough on that subject for the present. "Let's go round the rest of the house first."

The next door we tried was locked.

"Strange," said Fanny. "None of the other doors are locked." She tugged at the handle but it wouldn't give and when we squinted through the keyhole we saw nothing but blackness.

We went upstairs and did a tour of the bedrooms and maids' rooms. Fanny examined the portraits on the walls and recognised some.

"That's Grandfather as a young man," she said, pointing. He looked very upright. With a large moustache. "We have one like it at home. And there's Great-Uncle Jack!" He had a glint in his eye. "He was reckless, Fyffie says. You must meet Fyffie. But of course you can't, can you?"

We went down the stairs and tried the locked door again, just to make sure.

"We could go and look in through the window," I said.

"So we could. It's between the games room and the study, right?"

Fanny went out first to make sure it was safe for me to come out. When I heard her whistle I followed.

We peered through the windows, seeing from the outside all the rooms we had visited inside. The games room window was set high, we had to scramble up on to the sill to look in. Then we jumped down and went to the next window. We were by now round the side of the house and well hidden by large clumps of rhododendron.

This window was placed well above the ground, too. We climbed up.

"The curtains are drawn," said Fanny, disappointed.

We checked the next again window to see if it was the study. It was. We returned to the other one and stood on the ground below gazing up.

"Curiouser and curiouser," said Fanny. "The door is locked and the curtains are drawn!"

13

A Picnic in the Wood

It was all very mysterious: a house that had been locked up for thirty years and one of the rooms inside it locked and curtained.

"What exactly does your grandfather say when you ask him about the house?"

"He just says he doesn't want to talk about it. And he gets all worked up though he tries not to show it."

"Why don't you ask Fyffie?"

"She says her lips are sealed. And that I'm not to pester Grandpa or it'll make his blood pressure rise."

We returned to the house, to the kitchen, where we drank some orange juice. Our investigations had made us thirsty.

"Why don't you ask some of the people in the village?" I suggested.

"Don't you think I have?"

"And none of them'll talk, either?"

Fanny shook her head. "Perhaps you could ask at the shop? Mrs McWhirter's been here all her life. She'd know if anybody would."

"But I'm not supposed to be here."

"You needn't say you're staying in the house. You could be passing through."

I had to tell Fanny then that the police would be looking for me, that I was on the run.

"Gosh, your family does have an interesting time!"

Without lying, I was able to say the same about hers!

We laughed and Fanny asked me if I had any more secrets up my sleeve? I shook the sleeve of my tee-shirt. (And realised how grubby it was, though Fanny didn't appear to notice, or if she did, to mind. Her dress was very clean but then she had Fyffie to do her washing.)

"Not at the moment," I said.

"In that case, why don't we go for our picnic?"

Again, she went out ahead of me. I suddenly remembered something. Somebody.

"I'll only be a second, Fanny. I just want to check that Gully's all right."

"Gully?"

"Gulliver. My bike." We'd passed him earlier in the passage. I thought I'd heard him sniff as we went by.

"Oh, okay, I'll wait for you round the back."

Gulliver was sulking. "So you're going on a picnic without me, are you?"

"I can't take you, Gully. Look, how can I? We're going somewhere tucked away. You might not even be able to get there."

"I don't know what you want to be bothered with *her* for. Silly girls!"

"She's interesting."

Gulliver snorted.

I took hold of his handlebars and wheeled him along the corridor.

"Changing your mind, are you?"

"No, I'm not. I'm going to put you in a cupboard."

"A cupboard? In the dark?"

"Only till I come back." I was worried in case anyone might come into the house and find him standing in the hall. I opened the door of a cupboard that was half full of brooms and shovels and old cloths. There was just room for a bicycle. "It's for your own good."

"Your good, you mean!" said Gulliver. "Hey, I thought I was meant to be a freedom machine!"

"See you later," I said firmly, putting him inside and closing the door. Then I ran out into the sunshine to where Fanny was waiting with the picnic basket.

We crossed the field at the back of the house and went into a thick pine forest. Fanny told me it belonged to her grandfather and that we could be fairly certain of having it to ourselves.

We took a central path for half a mile or so before turning off on to a smaller track. The high trees cut the sun off from us now. We saw two red squirrels and a magpie and lots of chubby-looking chaffinches, and then a cock pheasant with a jewel green breast ran out in front of us. There were deer in the woods too, said Fanny, but they were probably up on the hill while the weather was good.

"It would be nice to live here all year round," I said.

I told her how my father had been brought up in the country but my mother preferred the town. Fanny was easy to tell things to. Things I wouldn't even have said to Pete.

We came to a clearing. The sun reached over the tops of the trees again. In fact, it was almost overhead. It must be midday.

A narrow burn flowed through the clearing and beside it stood the ruin of a small building.

"It used to be a kind of summerhouse," said Fanny, "It was built by my great-grandfather. They came here for family picnics. That's when there were lots of people living in the big house. Nobody uses it now. Except me."

"Where do you live, Fanny?" It had just struck me that I didn't know. "In the village?"

"No, we have another house in the grounds. A smaller one. It was kept for visitors until the family moved in thirty years ago."

We sat down beside the burn, with our backs against the old summerhouse wall. The place did have a nice tucked-away feel and Gulliver would not have been able to get here all that easily. The last part of the track had been rough and he might have got a puncture or had his paint scraped. I would tell him so when I got back.

Fanny spread out the food on a cloth. My mother likes to set a picnic out nicely, too, when we go for one. She seemed a long way away and it seemed a long time since I had seen her, even though it was less than three days. Could it be as little as that? I'd last seen her on Friday evening and this was Monday morning. I'd never known so much could happen to anyone in three days.

"What's up?" asked Fanny.

"Nothing."

"Your face looked sort of sad for a minute there."

"I was just wondering how my mother is. She has to have an operation, you see."

"My mother had one last year. And she got better very quickly."

"Did she?"

I cheered up and enjoyed my lunch. We ate everything. Fyffie could cook, all right. Fanny said she would bring some supper over to the house for me later.

"I'll sneak into the larder when Fyffie's out. This is her night for visiting her sister."

And what about Fanny's parents? I asked if she ever saw them?

"They come home in August every year. And I fly out for the Christmas holidays."

"Don't you mind — not seeing them all the times in between?"

"You get used to it. Don't you? Well, your father's away too, isn't he?"

I nodded. Yes, I was getting used to it.

"And I've got Grandpa and Fyffie."

It was very warm and the air felt heavy as if a thunderstorm might be brewing. We didn't feel like doing anything very much. We slid further down the bank and let our feet float in the cool burn water. I wondered if there were any fish in it.

"Quite a few. Nice brown trout."

"Do you fish?"

"Yes."

I would have been surprised except that by now I was

ceasing to be surprised by Fanny. I knew that I could not guess what she would say or do.

"We'll need to go out fishing together," she said. "Some evening. It wouldn't be any good with this sun overhead. How long are you going to stay?"

"I don't know. I haven't thought." I had planned to push on further north but now I was not so sure. The house, after all, was such a good hiding place. "Very good", I could hear Gulliver saying inside my head, "especially when you can shove me into a nasty dark cupboard! How would you like to be shut up with a lot of old brooms and shovels?" He can go on at times.

"Take each day as it comes," said Fanny. "That's what Fyffie says."

That was just what I had been doing, I said. Each hour, in fact.

"Do you know, I think I'll try asking Grandpa about the house again. Now that I've been inside it I feel I've *got* to know. I keep thinking about it and wondering."

For a few minutes we watched a kingfisher balancing on a low branch close to the water. We stayed very still until he went swooping off further down the burn.

"It must be great to be able to fly," I said.

"If we had wings we could go soaring high above the trees. We could go anywhere we wanted."

Right then, though, I was quite happy to be where I was.

"Do you go and visit your father in prison, Mungo? Do you mind me asking questions?"

I answered no to both questions.

"Why don't you go? Don't they allow children in?

"Oh, they do, but I don't want to go. Why should I? After what he did?"

"You're getting angry again," said Fanny.

I pulled my feet out of the burn and stood up. I turned to look back at the clearing. Standing beside the summerhouse wall, watching us, was an elderly man with a large white moustache.

14

Grandpa

I didn't have to be too smart to know who the man was. The painting of him in the house had been done a long time ago but the eyebrows were still heavy and the moustache the same shape. The only difference was that his hair was white. And his back was no longer so straight. He was slightly stooped, but not much.

I nudged Fanny with my foot and she, too, looked round.

"Grandpa!" she cried, leaping to her feet. It was the first time I'd seen her flustered.

"Hello, Fanny." He took a couple of steps towards us and I saw that he had two dogs at his heels. Springer spaniels.

"Romulus! Remus!" called Fanny and they came running to her. She patted them and they wagged their tails and licked her hands. I thought she was glad to have them to fuss over.

I wished I had something to fuss over. I kept my eyes on the dogs but I could feel Grandpa's fixed on me. He had given me a long, hard look as he stepped forward. What should I do? Make a dash for it? But I'd have to run all the way to the house first — and maybe he'd send the dogs after me! — climb in by the window, get Gulliver out of the cupboard and push him to the front door before I could start making my escape. Now if I'd had Gulliver with me I could have taken off straight-away. "Told you you shouldn't have left me behind, didn't I?" Oh, yes, I could hear him telling me that only too well.

The dogs were running in circles round Fanny now.

"You're getting them too excited, Fanny," said her grandfather gently and called them to heel. He looked at the empty basket. "Have you been having a picnic? Mrs Fyffie told me she'd packed a lunch for you."

"Yes. It was lovely. We had chicken and apple pie —"

"Aren't you going to introduce me to your friend?"

"Grandpa, this is —" She hesitated for just a second and then said quickly, "Gully."

"Hello, Gully. I'm pleased to meet you." The old man held out his hand and I took it and muttered something, I don't know what. I thought he was probably too polite to say, "Gully? That's a funny name. Is it short for something?" He said, "You're not local, are you?"

"No."

Fanny cut in. "He's staying in the caravan park at Long Brae."

"On holiday, then?"

"Yes," I said. He would think me a right idiot, not able to say anything but yes or no. I felt as if my tongue was stuck to the roof of my mouth. And I was still thinking about running, trying to work out how long it would take me to get to the house and bring Gulliver out.

"With your family?"

"Yes."

"His mother and father and two sisters," said Fanny. She smoothed her hair back from her forehead. Little beads of sweat stood out round the hairline and she was very pink in the cheeks. I had a feeling that she didn't often tell lies. And that her grandfather would know she was telling one now. But it was me he was still looking at.

"Enjoying it here, are you?" he asked.

"Yes."

"Good. I think I'll be getting back to the house. Will you be coming soon, Fanny?"

"In a few minutes."

"Don't be long, then. Nice to meet you, Gully."

"Cheerio," I croaked.

He went back into the wood, followed by the dogs. Fanny and I stood listening to the rustle of their feet. We didn't move until the only thing we could hear was the cry of the birds again.

"Whew!" said Fanny and bending over, wiped her forehead with the edge of her skirt.

"Do you think he was suspicious?"

"I don't think he'd suspect who you are. Why should he? He mightn't even have seen anything about you in the papers."

I imagined that everyone in the world must know about me but maybe she was right.

"He didn't like you being with me, though, did he?" I scuffed the dry grass on the bank with my toes. "Probably thought I was a tramp or something." I couldn't really blame him if he did but I knew that I was trying to, in a funny sort of way.

"Don't worry, though, Mungo. He won't go down to the caravan park to check, I'm sure he won't."

But I couldn't help worrying and the afternoon had changed. The place no longer felt tucked away and we no longer felt lazy and peaceful. Fanny waded up the burn and I sat on the bank pulling up handfuls of grass.

"Those were nice dogs," I said. My father had always wanted to have a dog but how could we, in our small flat? It was all right for Fanny and her grandfather with their big houses and their fields and woods. "Does he go hunting with them?"

"Oh no! Grandpa hates hunting. He would never kill anything."

She came out of the water. She sighed. "I think I'd better be getting home."

"Yes," I said.

She picked up the basket and we trudged in silence back along the path. We paused on the edge of the wood and looked across the field. There was no sign of anyone about but Fanny said she'd better go in front anyway to make sure.

"I'll bring your supper over later."

"Oh, okay. But don't bother if you can't."

She went ahead.

"Fanny," I called.

She looked back.

"It was a nice picnic."

She nodded.

I had no trouble getting back into the house. And Gulliver was as I'd left him.

"Who did you think was going to nick me? And I couldn't run off on my own, could I? More's the pity! I hope you had a good time? You and your fancy friends!"

"They can't help being fancy. Anyway, they're not what you'd really call *fancy*."

Fancy was one of Aunt Janet's words. "You and your fancy ideas!" she would say to my father when he talked about his schemes for travelling round the world. We would sell the flat and buy a bus and take off, all five of us, and go wherever the fancy took us. Yes, fancy. He used it that time. "And what will you do for money when you get back?" Aunt Janet had asked. "And where will you live?" But I had noticed that while my dad — *father* — was talking my mother's eyes had been lit up and although she had shaken her head she had laughed too.

I took Gulliver out of the cupboard and to give him some exercise rode him round the hall and up the passages.

"This isn't much fun," he grumbled. "I could be doing with some fresh air."

But I didn't want to risk being seen outside.

Gulliver was right — it wasn't a lot of fun trying to cycle in such a tight space, especially when I felt like getting my head down and pushing the pedals round as fast as I could. I was restless. I put Gulliver back in the cupboard.

"I suppose this is for my own good again?"

"Just in case anyone comes in." I felt extra cautious

since I'd met Fanny's grandfather. I'd seen the look in his eye. He'd been having a good think about me.

"Why don't we take off, then?" said Gulliver. "Head further north, like we planned?"

"I couldn't do that, not without —"

"Saying goodbye to Miss Fanny!"

I shut the door on him.

I went upstairs to my room. It was beginning to feel like my room. I stared again at the picture of the two girls. Fanny *did* look very like both of them. When I looked into their faces I felt as if I were looking into hers. I wondered when she would come. She would have to have her supper first and Fyffie would have to go out. It would not be for a while.

Time seemed to have stopped. I was surprised when I looked at my watch to see the second hand still working its way round the face. Five to five. The room was stuffy. I pushed the window up a little way. Nothing moved on either the drive or the road beyond. I gazed at the hills and wished I were up there walking through the bracken and heather. I thought of the birds trapped in the turret. I thought of my father trapped in his cell.

Then I shook myself and, going to the gramophone, wound it up and put on a record, 'The Bonny Bonny Banks of Loch Lomond', keeping the sound down low.

> You'll tak' the high road and I'll tak' the low road,
> And I'll be in Scotland before you . . .

Even that amount of sound seemed too much in this big, still house. When the record finished I didn't play another but went to lie on my bed and read *Gulliver's*

Travels. And after a page or so I fell asleep. Which is what Gulliver did after he'd been shipwrecked and swam ashore at Lilliput. And again I had that dream of being pinned to the ground by cords and not able to get up.

But when I'd pulled myself together after I awoke — and that was just what it felt like — I did get up and I saw that it was nine o'clock. I had thought Fanny would have come long before this. Perhaps she was not going to come after all. Perhaps she'd thought I'd not been very nice to her after her grandfather left us. And when she'd said she'd bring my supper over I had said, "Don't bother if you can't." So if she was not going to bother it would just be hard cheese for me.

I could have been doing with some cheese, hard or not. My tummy was making noises to tell me it needed something to keep it quiet. I only had a few nuts and raisins left. The last piece of chocolate had melted and messed up the panier. I ate the nuts and rasins quickly and was still hungry. The mushroom book caught my eye but it didn't seem very practical to start hunting for mushrooms — or berries — at this time of night.

There was tinned food in the pantry, I remembered, and went down to inspect it more closely. I found an ancient rusty tin opener and cut a jagged hole in a tin of peaches. They didn't smell too good and the inside of the tin looked black. I left them. Better to be hungry than poisoned. And I might roll around in agony for days in here without anyone coming to my rescue. Fanny might not come back again, ever.

I went back upstairs to see if I'd missed any food in

either of the two paniers. I found two peanuts and a hazelnut. Big deal! I demolished them and tried not to think of fish and chips or toasted cheese or even just plain toast.

"Come on, Fanny, if you're coming!" I said out loud and crossed to the window to see if she was.

And I saw, not Fanny, but her grandfather.

15

The Locked Room Unlocked

He was coming up the drive towards the front door! He must have seen me on my way back into the house. Perhaps he had waited at the edge of the wood with his hands on the dogs' heads so that they would be quiet, and watched.

What should I do? For a moment I was in a real panic. I thought the game was up. He would track me down, I couldn't see how he wouldn't. Then I remembered that Gulliver was hidden away and was glad of that, at least. And remembering that brought me to my senses. I must hide too.

I could no longer see him when I looked down. He must be in the porch. There was no time to waste. The heavy front door thudded shut below.

But where should I hide? "Don't just stand there!" Gulliver would growl. The toy box was too small and full of toys. The wardrobe was too narrow and full of clothes. The one cupboard in the room was only a shelf wide and full of things like paints and crayons and drawing books even if I could have squeezed myself in.

He was coming up the stairs. I dived under the nearest bed. And sneezed. And sneezed again, silently. I had never realised before that you don't have to make a noise when you sneeze. I listened to my heart going bump, bump, bump.

He was opening the door. I pinched my nose to stop myself sneezing again. I thought I would choke. The floor was shaking. He was walking around. Stopping now. Walking again. A few steps at a time. I could see nothing because of the bedcover which hung right down to the floor.

He had stopped again and for what seemed like for ever nothing at all happened. I waited for him to lift the bedcover and find me. The waiting was so terrible that I almost crept out and gave myself up.

He sighed. Perhaps he was looking at the photographs of the two girls. He must be sad that Jane had died. Although it *was* a very long time ago. But I supposed that, even so, he would still be sad when he thought of her. My mum says there are some things you never get over. Her mum had died when she was young and she said she had never really got over that, which didn't mean she was sad all the time or even much of the time. Would I ever get over what my dad — *father* — had done?

"Of course he always worshipped his father, didn't he?" Aunt Janet said on one of her visits when she and my mum were discussing how *difficult* I had become. The thing is that when she said it she sounded smug, as if she'd always known we were headed for disaster.

I felt as if I were heading for disaster now. The inside of my nose was prickling like mad. A sneeze was building up. What was Grandpa doing? Had he turned into a statue?

Then I felt a vibration in the floor again and his footsteps moved away, towards the door. He opened it and went out, shutting it behind him. I couldn't believe it. I stayed still for another minute or two in case it was a trick. But it seemed that he was going back downstairs. I let my sneeze out. What a relief! I didn't even care about the noise.

I wriggled like a crab from my hiding place. I was covered with dust. Thirty years of the stuff, from the looks of it. Aunt Janet has said more than once that I only have to look at dirt and it sticks to me. My dad — *father*, for goodness sake! — would say, once she'd gone, that she didn't know anything about kids.

"Why does she come here?" he'd ask my mother.

"She's fond of the children, you know, underneath."

A thousand fathoms down.

Giving myself a quick brush off, I went to the door and eased it open. I listened. Fanny's grandfather was walking about downstairs, walking very slowly, it seemed to me. Not like a man who was looking for something. Or somebody. More like a man who was just looking around. I began to feel better. He might not be hunting for me after all.

I crept out on to the landing and made my way along to the top of the stairs.

Inside the big, high house it was dusk. When I had looked out of the window it had still been a summer evening, but in here there was hardly any light and the place was full of shadows. My ears would be of more use than my eyes.

99

To them came the rustle of the birds overhead and the slow drag of the old man's footsteps from below. Surely Gulliver was right — this must be a haunted house? I even wondered if the old man was real. His footsteps sounded more like those of a ghost's. But Fanny had been real enough, I reminded myself. "Too real," said Gulliver in the cupboard downstairs. "Pity she hadn't been a ghost. Ghosts don't go for picnics." I told him to shut up.

But where *was* Fanny? And why *hadn't* she come?

I began to inch my way down the stairs, keeping close to the wall. My shoulder caught an ancestor portrait and sent it askew. I straightened it. The only sound to be heard now was that made by the birds. I ran the rest of the way down the stairs.

Grandpa had vanished down one of the passages. He must have gone into a room. He might be standing inside it, standing and staring, the way he had in the girls' room upstairs. I thought I knew which room he would be in.

Up ahead, I saw a light flickering. He must have a torch. In a second I was inside the cupboard with Gulliver.

"Watch what you're doing! You're trampling on me. How would you like it if I was to cycle all over the top of you?"

"Shush!"

"I won't shush. What do you think you're playing at? Cops and robbers?"

I did feel a bit like a cop — a Private Eye, that is — but I wasn't going to admit it to Gulliver. There was some sort of mystery locked up in that room and I was determined to find out what it was. I was listening to the old man's footsteps as they came nearer and nearer. And then passed by. On their way to the front door.

It was stifling inside the cupboard and the old brooms and cloths smelt pretty awful.

"Told you it wasn't nice in here, didn't I?" said Gulliver. "Do you good — to get some of your own medicine."

The footsteps had stopped again. A door was opening, but not the front one. It sounded more like a cupboard. I had an idea which cupboard it might be. There was a small one high up on the wall beside the front door. And was that the clink of keys? I had never checked that cupboard. I felt myself getting excited.

And then the front door banged shut. We felt the tremble of it right through to our hiding place. I opened the cupboard door and took a deep breath.

"I hope you're going to get me out of here now," said Gulliver.

"I can't, not just yet. I'm going to light a candle."

"Pity you had to leave the torch behind!"

That was one of Gulliver's remarks which I ignored. I fumbled my way into the kitchen and found the matches Fanny had brought and lit a candle.

The flame guided me to the little cupboard beside the front door. My fingers trembled as I took hold of the handle and tugged it open. Inside, hanging on a nail, was a bunch of keys!

I took them down and went back to wave them in front of Gulliver's nose.

"Look what I found!"

"I know what you're up to, Mungo McKinnon! Just watch yourself, that's all! A spookie might get you. Or you might fall over a dead body."

"It would be a skeleton by now. After thirty years."

With the light wavering in front of me looking very like a ghost's candle, I went along the passage to the locked room.

I examined the lock and then the keys to see which ones would be likely to fit. There were four of about the right size. The first two wouldn't turn. The third one did.

I pushed open the door and put one foot across the threshold. The candlelight flickered over the walls, showing what kind of room it was. It was a gun room.

16

A Night Storm

Guns covered the walls. Sporting rifles. I guessed,
though I didn't know much about them. Nothing at all,
really. They were not hung up any old way but arranged
so that they made neat patterns. It was odd, wasn't it, to
have a whole roomful of guns when you didn't like
shooting? But perhaps Fanny's grandfather had inher-
ited the guns with the house and had kept the room as a
kind of museum.

I walked slowly round the edges of the room
until I came to the fourth wall. The pattern was
broken here. There was a space. One gun was
missing!

I felt a tingle run up my back bone. But it might *not*
mean anything. The gun might have been missing for
years and years. But what if the old man had taken it
down when he came into the room? What if he was
wandering about with it right now? What if he'd gone a
bit loopy in the head? Sometimes people do terrible
things then. I thought of Fanny. What if he were to . . . ?
My imagination was running away with me. Too much
imagination . . . .

Yes, all right, Aunt Janet! For once, though, I thought
she might be right.

"You must be getting soft in the head," said Gulliver,

back in his cupboard, "if you're starting to think Aunt Janet could be right about anything."

I did feel a bit soft in the head. I had to get out of this room. It was making me feel very odd.

"And, all right, Gully, you don't have to say it!"

I backed out of the room. It had bad vibes, that was for sure. I was glad when I was on the other side of the door. Standing in there I'd felt almost as if bolts of electricity were being shot through me. I'd felt slightly sick. I could have been doing with some ordinary electricity in the light bulbs. This candlelight was far too creepy and every now and then the flame spluttered and almost died. I remembered when we'd had a power cut at home and had had to make do with candles. I'd enjoyed that. But that had been different: we'd all been together.

What was that? I stopped to listen. I thought I'd heard a new noise in the house. The place seemed to be creaking and groaning more than ever tonight. I went back to Gulliver.

"So what good did all that do you? Curiosity killed the cat, eh?"

It didn't kill me. I'm still here. And I'm going to bed."

I wanted to get my head down and fall asleep and not waken until it was broad daylight.

"Don't tell me you're cracking up!"

"Cracking up nothing! I'm tired. Goodnight, Gully."

On the way up the stairs the candle blew out. And I'd left the matches down in the kitchen. I was too tired to go and fetch them. I crawled up the rest of the stairs holding on to the bannister rail.

As I came in to my room a flash of lightning lit it up. A roll of thunder followed. That was what the noise had been that I'd heard. It looked like we were in for a storm after all.

I love good-going thunderstorms. As long as I can watch them from somewhere safe. I don't want to lie in the middle of an open field or anything stupid like that and when Billy bet me I wouldn't sit under a tree by the Water of Leith during a storm I didn't do it. He was pretty stupid, now I came to think about him, and when I went back home I was going to ignore him. I didn't *have* to go around with him just because I always had. The lightning came again and bang! went the thunder. The twins hate storms and always go into our mum's big bed and huddle under the covers. I wriggled into my sleeping bag but stayed sitting up. I no longer felt soft in the head or scared or even tired.

The lightning flashed and the thunder banged. I counted between the flashes and the bangs. One, two, three — four! So the centre of the storm was four miles away. One, two — three! It was coming closer. I wondered if Fanny would be watching. I didn't think anyone could sleep through noise like this. Would she be with her grandfather? Before I could start wondering about the missing gun again the next flash came, making the room look bright as midday, and I could see the two girls, Fanny and Jane, in their silver frames. One, two — crash! Fanny and Jane didn't even blink.

Now I counted to one and the thunder rolled. Another flash — no time to count — the thunder was coming, booming, shaking the house, deafening my ears. I held them flat to my head with my hands. The flashes and bangs were tremendous. The storm must be right overhead. I'd never seen one like it before.

It raged for perhaps ten minutes before gradually moving away, still grumbling and growling like some huge beast. A real Gulliver of a storm.

Tomorrow I must take my Gulliver for a ride out in the fresh air. For the rain would come and the air would surely be fresh after that. As I drifted into sleep I thought of the birds. What would the blinding light have done to them? Would it have sent them mad and made them hurl themselves at the window again and again, getting into a bigger and bigger frenzy every time the lightning sizzled? The trapped birds came with me into my dreams. As did my trapped father. He seemed to be standing in the middle of the turret, with his arms across his face trying to protect it from the birds who were whirling round and round him.

In spite of my nightmare, I awoke in the morning with a clear head. And I knew there was something I had to do and that I must do it before my nerve failed.

There wasn't as much noise as usual coming from the turret. The sounds were quieter, less hectic. I hoped my friend the bat would be kipping. Upside down, in the turret roof, far above my head.

Outside the door I paused to take a big breath, then I opened it and marched in. The room was darker than I'd expected, than it had been on my last visit. Then I heard the drumming of the rain on the roof. When I had wakened my mind had not been on the weather.

Two birds were flying about, another two were on the floor fluttering a bit. I didn't wait to see where the bat was. I took a firm hold of one of the birds on the floor. Its heart beat madly under my fingers as I carried it to the hole in the window and my feet scrunched on the dead birds and skeletons of dead birds. The noise was horrible and made my stomach flip right over. I swallowed. And kept going. Don't look down! I told myself, *don't!* I put my hand out and opened my fingers.

To begin with the bird dropped and my heart did too, then its wings quivered and rose and away it flew. I gave a small cheer, a very feeble one, for I wasn't in much of a cheering mood. The second one was also easy to free but the two that were flying about gave me more trouble. After a few goes I caught number three but number four, a fat swallow, didn't want to co-operate at all. He soared and swooped and divebombed me and went wild against the window until he had me sweating and on the point of giving up. For a moment though he settled and *I* swooped. He went quiet in my hand, except for his heart.

When I'd sent him on his way I noticed a small bird moving on the floor. He was just alive but would never fly again. One wing was broken. I looked round for a heavy object and found a lump of broken plaster. I hit the bird over the head. Nothing else stirred in the room. If the bat was up there he'd have to take his chances. Bats can slip in and out of very narrow slits, I remembered my dad — all right then, *dad*! — telling me. He'd also said he didn't wish bats any harm even though one had once got tangled in his hair. He thought they were interesting creatures. This wasn't the time for me to get interested in them — that would have to wait. I took the piece of thick cardboard I'd brought with me and rammed it into the hole in the window.

Mission completed, I got out of there as fast as I could.

When I had closed the door behind me, I surveyed my feet. My gym shoes were covered with bits of bone and bird feathers. I ran down the twisty staircase to the nearest lavatory and was sick.

As I surfaced to wash my face, I heard Fanny calling me.

17

Secrets

"Mungo!"

"I'm here. I'm coming."

We met at the top of the stairs. She was wearing jeans and an anorak and her hair was dark with rain. My hair was wet too, from the water I'd sluiced over it. And my feet were bare. I'd dumped the gym shoes.

"I was beginning to think you'd gone." She stared at me. "You look awfully pale."

So did she. I said so.

"What about me?" said Gulliver, from his cupboard. "Don't you think I look pale, too? I won't exactly get a tan lying in here. I haven't seen daylight for nearly twenty-four hours. And the smell isn't getting any better."

"I've got lots to tell you," said Fanny.

"So have I."

"Let's go down to the kitchen. I've brought you some breakfast."

On the way past Gulliver's cupboard I took a quick look in. He was right about the smell.

"Don't mind me," he said.

I made a face at him, then hurried after Fanny. She was unpacking from a plastic carrier bag a thermos of hot tea, two bacon rolls and some fruit.

"That was all I could manage this time, I'm afraid. Fyffie was bustling about rather a lot."

"That's brilliant."

The tea was what I most wanted. I drank a whole mugful before I turned to the food.

"Your colour's coming back," said Fanny.

I told her about the birds and she shivered.

"That was very brave of you."

I thought it was *quite* brave myself although I said it was nothing. It wasn't something I'd want to do every morning before breakfast. I took a bite of one of the bacon rolls.

"This isn't your breakfast, is it, Fanny?"

"No, no," she said and I saw that it was, but she insisted that I carry on. "I get plenty to eat. I'm terribly sorry I didn't come last night, Mungo. You must have been starving?"

"I was all right."

"Fyffie didn't go out, you see."

"Why was that?"

"Something about her sister having a headache — I didn't believe it."

"Do you think your grandfather had warned her about me?"

"I don't know about warned . . . ." Fanny shrugged. "He may have *said* something. Anyway, she didn't leave me alone for a second all evening. If I as much as moved she asked where I was going."

"Your grandfather came here."

"I know. He told me."

That did surprise me.

"I asked him about the house when I came in from the picnic. I pleaded with him to talk to me about it and I thought he was going to, then he changed his mind. And later on he went out."

"Did he tell you what he came to the house for?"

"To look round, he said. To try to lay old ghosts."

I had finished the second bacon roll and was swallowing the last mouthful of tea. I got up.

"He came for more than that. Come on, Fanny, I'll show you!"

She followed me into the hall and I took the keys from the small cupboard. Her dark blue eyes went very wide. We hurried along the passage to the locked room and I unlocked it.

"Wait a minute!" I said. "Wait there!" Leaving her on the threshold, I went boldly into the room and drew back the curtains. In the daytime, and with Fanny there, I wasn't so worried about my head softening up. She was hesitating in the doorway. "You can come in now."

She came slowly in, glancing nervously at the walls.

"Guns!" I said, as if she couldn't see.

"Yes, I know."

"Did he fill you in on them, too?"

She nodded.

The morning was turning out to be full of surprises. I showed her the broken pattern on the wall. "He took that one down."

"No, he didn't. At least not last night. The last time he took it down was thirty years ago. Listen! I'll tell you what he told me." She lowered her voice and while she was speaking she went on looking around as if she half expected someone else to be listening, too.

"Fanny," he had said, "I am going to let you in on the house's secret. It's about time I did. *My* secret. It's a very sad one."

I was beginning to feel less bold. And the room was beginning to feel eerie again.

"He had been out shooting," said Fanny, "and had just come back. He was in here cleaning the gun. That gun!" She pointed to the empty space.

"I thought he hated hunting?"

"He did — after what happened in here that day." Her voice trembled. "Oh, it was awful, Mungo!"

I put my arm around her shoulder, I had to, to make her feel better.

"Naturally," said Gulliver, from his dark place.

Well, why shouldn't I?

"You'd better tell me the rest, Fanny."

"He'd forgotten to take out the remaining cartridge before he started to clean it. He should have done. It's dangerous not to."

"And someone came in?"

"Yes. It was my aunt —"

"Jane?"

"Yes. The gun went off and killed her. She was only ten. *My* age. It was an accident." Fanny was crying now and I could feel a fairly big lump bothering me at the back of my throat.

"No wonder he locked the house up after that," I said.

"It's a wonder he didn't move away to somewhere else."

"He couldn't really have done that. Our family has lived here for hundreds of years."

We didn't speak for a moment and I thought about the two girls in their silver frames. "I'm glad it was Jane and not Fanny who was killed."

"Oh, they wouldn't have called me after the dead girl." Fanny was shivering so much that her teeth were chattering. "Poor, poor Grandpa, he made a mistake and he's had to live with it for the rest of his life. That's what Fyffie says."

"It must have been pretty terrible." Worse than embezzling, I couldn't help thinking, and felt a bit selfish even to be thinking about myself and my own family at this time.

"Mungo!" said Fanny sharply. She was facing the window. She had gone very pale again.

I turned to see what it was that was upsetting her. Outside, in the steadily falling rain, looking in on us, was her grandfather.

Should I make a run for it?

"Better be quick if you're going to," said Gulliver, from the cupboard. "I'm ready and willing."

But I had had enough of running and hiding. I stood my ground.

18

We See the Ghost

"I think we'd better go over to the house," said Fanny's grandfather, "where it's more comfortable. And then you can tell me all about yourself."

The house — the one they lived in — was about a mile away. We went in Grandpa's Range Rover. None of us said much during the short ride down the drive and along the road. Grandpa said something about it being a pity that the weather had broken, but that was all. I felt very calm inside. And I was glad of the sound of the rain on the car roof. It filled up the silences.

We pulled up in front of a good-sized house (it turned out to have five bedrooms) standing by itself on the edge of the estate. Red virginia creeper half-covered the stone walls and the garden was full of dahlias and roses. It had a much friendlier look about it than the other house with its towers and turrets.

Fyffie came out to meet us. She was small and round and looked much as I'd expected. I'd have been disappointed if she'd turned out to be long and skinny. "Come away in and I'll make you all a nice pot of tea," she said. "I've just taken a batch of fresh scones from the oven. Or would you rather have cocoa, the two of you? You look gey peely-wally." She clucked at Fanny.

We sat in the kitchen where a fire crackled in the grate.

Fyffie gave it a stir up and went out leaving us, with our hot drinks and soft warm scones.

"Now then?" said Grandpa, fixing me with a stare that was rather like Fanny's. His eyes were more or less the same colour, or would have been when he was young.

Fanny jumped in quickly to say that my name was not Gully. From afar, I heard Gulliver sniff. Fanny was blushing. "I was just trying to throw you off the scent, Grandpa."

"So what is your name then?"

"Mungo McKinnon."

"Why don't you begin at the beginning, Mungo, and tell me the whole story?"

So I did and I told him everything.

"You've had quite a time of it, haven't you?" he said, when I'd come to the end of my story, or the story as it was so far, for I knew it was not yet ended. He sat quiet for a bit, fiddling with his moustaches. Fanny and I eyed one another, waiting to hear what he would say. I knew of course that he *would* say that he'd have to get in touch with my mother. I couldn't expect him not to. I couldn't expect him to hide me.

"You've got spunk, Mungo."

"Thank you." I wondered if I should call him sir but I couldn't quite get it out.

"Will you telephone your mother or shall I?"

"Would you?"

He nodded. "Yes, I think I could put your case better. And she won't get so worked up if I speak to her, will she?" He smiled. "In the meantime, why don't you stay here with us? I don't suppose you'd want to spend another night over there?"

"Not particularly."

"Thanks, Grandpa," said Fanny.

He patted the top of her head and I thought how hard it must be for him to see her and be reminded all the time of Jane.

I gave him my phone number and he went off to his study to make the call. Fanny and I watched the flames in the fire.

"I don't suppose your mother will be too angry, do you? She'll probably be relieved more."

Grandpa came back to say there had been no answer.

"She might be out at the shops. Or in the hospital," I added, and my heart fluttered, reminding me of the birds in the turret. "She might have gone in for her operation."

"In that case, perhaps I should phone your aunt?"

"Do you have to?"

"I'm afraid so."

I told him the number and he went away again.

"*She* won't be relieved," I said.

"She can't eat you," said Fanny.

"Want to bet? She's got teeth like a crocodile." I opened my mouth and made a snapping sound with my teeth. At least it made us laugh.

"She might let you stay with us. I mean, if she doesn't want to have you yourself . . . ."

But that would be too good to come true. Aunt Janet would have me to stay with her even if it killed her. And me. She would have to do her duty. "Stay with people we don't know? Oh no, Mungo, we can't have that. We don't take favours from strangers. We don't need to take favours from anybody." I could hear her voice running on in my head.

Grandpa had not come back this time. Aunt Janet must be at home. I sighed.

"I don't imagine she'd come today, do you?" said Fanny.

It had never occurred to me that Aunt Janet might actually come here. Perish the thought! as she herself would say. I didn't want her to come and meet Fanny and Grandpa and Fyffie and see the house, the two houses. I didn't want her busybody eyes flitting about noticing everything. This was *my* place. "She'd better not come!"

"But she won't let you go back home on your own, will she? After all, I don't suppose she'd —"

"Trust me?" Now I was feeling downright gloomy. "No, I don't suppose she would."

We looked round as the door opened. Grandpa rejoined us at the fire.

"I've spoken to your aunt and she's going to come tomorrow. I shall meet her off the train at Pitlochry. I've given her my word that you won't take off during the night. So I'll have to ask you, Mungo, to give me *your* word that you won't."

I hesitated for only a second — and thought of Gulliver lying in the dark cupboard waiting for me — and then I gave it. But I knew, as I did, that that would be the end of my freedom run.

117

"Good. I'll go and have a word with Fyffie about making up a room for you. And then we'll need to collect your things from the other house."

"We can do that, Grandpa," said Fanny. "You don't have to bother."

"There isn't much," I said. "It'll all go on the bike."

We had lunch before we went. It was the first proper hot meal I'd had since leaving home. Chicken and mushroom pie with new potatoes and fresh peas and home-grown strawberries with cream to follow!

"I like to see young folks enjoying their food," said Fyffie.

The rain had stopped by the time we set out. The trees looked fresh and raindrops glistened on the leaves. The top of the hill was hidden in cloud.

"Fanny," I said, "do you believe once a thief always a thief?"

"No, I don't. Why should it be once anything always anything? I hope it needn't be. I wouldn't want to be stuck for ever and ever as I am now. Would you?"

"No." Though I did wish that time would stand still, for once. But I knew there wasn't much chance of that.

The big house looked grim on this dark day as if it were telling us not to come inside. I think we both felt a bit shivery as we walked up the drive.

"It won't take more than five minutes to get my things together," I said.

It was dark in the hall. Fanny suggested we leave the front door open. I went at once to the cupboard and rescued Gulliver.

"About time too," he groused. "I've just about had enough of this lark."

Fanny and I went upstairs to the girls' bedroom. I packed my rucksack and rolled up my sleeping bag. Fanny stood in front of the photographs on the wall.

"I wonder which was Fanny and which was Jane," she said.

"It doesn't matter now, does it?"

"No, it doesn't."

We took a last look round then closed the door behind us.

"Shall we take a last look at the gun room, too?" said Fanny.

Outside the door she slipped her hand into mine. I was glad to have it to hold on to just as I suppose she was glad of mine.

We opened the door. Standing in the middle of the room was a girl in a pale dress. We saw her. We *definitely* saw her.

19

Aunt Janet Arrives

I didn't tell Aunt Janet about the ghost, of course. I'd heard what she had to say on the subject of the imagination often enough. Fanny and I hadn't told anyone. It would have upset her grandfather and Fyffie might not have let her out of her sight afterwards.

"She would believe us," said Fanny, "but she'd worry. It's not that Jane would do us any harm, I'm sure, but still —"

You don't really feel like hanging around when you've seen a ghost. We'd fled after we'd seen the girl in the light-coloured dress, stopping long enough only to pick up Gulliver. He'd grumbled about being jiggled and bounced down the front steps.

Aunt Janet sat in the sitting room of Fanny's house holding her handbag on her lap. She was wearing her best dress and she was amazingly quiet. I couldn't get over how quiet she was. It was Grandpa, I supposed, who was doing that to her.

The best news was that my mum had had her operation and was all right!

"Yes, she's doing very well," said Aunt Janet. "She was very relieved to hear that *you* were safe and sound, Mungo."

That didn't make me feel so good. And I didn't know

how safe or sound I was at that moment. I was sitting on the edge of my chair waiting for the storm to break over my head when Grandpa and Fanny would leave us alone. The lightning would flash and the thunder roll then! And when it was over I would have to put Gulliver into the back of the Range Rover and go home with Aunt Janet. I would have to say goodbye to Fanny.

She was very quiet, too. The only one with anything much to say was Grandpa.

"Well," he said, eventually, getting up, "shall we go and pick some strawberries for lunch, Fanny? You'll be lunching with us, I hope, Mrs Blair?"

"Thank you, that would be nice." She tightened her grip on the handbag.

"We'll see you later, then."

I didn't look at Aunt Janet's face. I parked my elbows on my knees and my head between my hands and stared down at the pattern on the carpet. There were trees and flowers and strange looking animals. It was Persian, Fanny said.

"Oh, Mungo!"

I looked up then. Aunt Janet had burst into tears. I just stared at her. I had never seen her *crying* before.

"I've felt terrible, you've no idea. To think I'd been so beastly to you that you'd run away rather than stay with me!"

I wanted to get out of there. And leap on my freedom machine. And take off. But all I could do was sit and gape.

"It's not true, Mungo — I don't hate you. We may

have had our differences but I've never *hated* you, honestly I haven't. You see, you don't understand."

It annoys me when grown-ups tell you you don't understand when they've not even told you what there is to understand.

Aunt Janet blew her nose and dried her eyes and sighed. "There's something I want to tell you." She paused. More secrets? It seemed that everyone had them, by the bushel. Skeletons rattling in closets all over the country. I waited. "I would have liked very much to have had children of my own but I wasn't able to."

"But Mum said you didn't want to have any?"

"That's what I've always told people. Well, you don't want them to see that you're —"

"Hurt," I said.

"That's right. You understand that, don't you, Mungo?"

I nodded. I understood it only too well.

"I was dying to have a baby so when you were born I suppose I resented it, which was stupid of me. But Margaret was younger than me and had always seemed to get what she wanted and here she was getting what she wanted again. I took it out on you, in a way. It was unforgivable of me."

Aunt Janet saying she was stupid! And had done something unforgivable. The world *was* turning itself upside down.

"Mungo, I'm so sorry."

"That's all right," I mumbled.

"But it's not, is it? Look what I drove you to do! It must have been awful for you."

No, awful was not the word I would have used. It had been frightening at times, and lonely, but not awful.

"It was lucky you fell in with such nice people."

That was something I could agree with. And Poppy had been nice, too, even though she'd phoned the police in the end. We'd had a jolly good time at the fair together. Sometime, perhaps, I might go back to Perth fair and look for her there.

"How did you feel, Mungo," asked Aunt Janet, "being away all on your own?"

"I was worried about my mum — that was the worst thing."

"I know, I know! As if she didn't have enough on her plate." Aunt Janet was screwing her hanky into a ball and clenching it in her fist. Her eyes looked sore. I thought she'd been doing quite a bit of crying even before she came here. I was beginning — yes, I was — to feel sorry for her.

"It's all right, Aunt Janet, really it is."

She looked straight at me and I didn't look away. "Can we start again, Mungo, you and I?"

Of course I said yes. Though I have to admit that I didn't relish the idea *too* much. She might try to be so nice to me it would become embarrassing. But maybe not. For once we got home and settled down she'd probably start warning me about the imagination again and cutting out my coat and all that. She was still Aunt Janet after all and she's the one who likes to say a leopard doesn't change its spots.

"Thank you, Mungo."

"How're the twins?" I asked, to get us on to a different tack.

"Very well. They send you their love. They were very upset, too, when you went, particularly Susie."

"Honest?"

"Of course they were! Didn't you think they would be? Susie cried herself to sleep every night."

I was quite pleased that she had, yet I felt bad about it too. Nothing seemed to be straightforward.

"And that reminds me —" Aunt Janet rummaged in her handbag which is the size of a sack and brought out a paper bag. She passed it across to me. "That's from them."

Inside was a packet of Smarties which didn't feel quite full and half a Mars bar and two cards made out of sugar paper. Susie had drawn a bike in green crayons and Cathy some yellow flowers (her favourite colour) and they had both written in straggly printing: COME HOME SOON. (Susie had missed the e off both come and home.) I swallowed. That silly lump had come out of nowhere again.

"Don't be so sloppy," said Gulliver from the shed in the garden where I'd parked him.

I put the cards and the chocolate back in the bag.

"That was nice of them," I said.

"They're really very sweet," said Aunt Janet.

"Sweet nothing," said Gulliver. "Just wait till you're

home a couple of days — they'll be driving you round the twist again."

"Oh, shut up, Gully! You know you like them all right yourself."

"Did you say something, Mungo?"

"No, nothing."

"What about showing me the garden? It looks beautifully kept."

We found Fanny and her grandfather in the kitchen garden. Aunt Janet admired all the fruit and vegetables and then she and Grandpa went back indoors to have a pow-wow. Fanny and I stayed beside the strawberry beds. We kept popping berries in our mouths, they looked so good.

"Your Aunt Janet isn't nearly as dreadful as I'd expected," said Fanny.

"She's not such a bad old stick."

Fanny raised an eyebrow.

I repeated the conversation I'd had with my aunt. Whom would I tell such things to when I went home?

"Remember me?" said Gulliver. "There was a time when you used to tell me everything."

"You can write letters to me," said Fanny. "Will you, Mungo? I love getting letters, especially when I'm at school. And I'll write back."

"Lunch," called Fyffie from the kitchen door. "And don't be eating any more of those berries or you'll spoil your appetites."

Lunch went off all right. Aunt Janet seemed to have cheered up and she enjoyed her meal. She praised every mouthful she ate before it had time to touch down, saying how marvellous it must be to live in the country and grow your own vegetables. She didn't look anywhere near me while she was saying it. She's as much a townee as my mum is. But I didn't mind her telling the odd little fib. She was just wanting to please.

"Absolutely delicious, Mrs Fyffe," she said, as she finished her wedge of strawberry shortcake and dabbed her mouth with her napkin.

"Another piece?"

"Well, I shouldn't really . . . I'm supposed to be on a diet." She laughed and held out her plate. "Only a sliver, then. I've never tasted such good strawberry shortcake."

"I could give you the recipe."

"Would you? That would be marvellous." (She can't bake for toffee, Aunt Janet. In fact, her baking, when she does do any, which isn't often, tastes very like toffee.) "And then I can make it for Mungo when we go home."

I had been about to pass up my plate for seconds but with the mention of going home my appetite vanished.

"Talking of that, Mrs Blair," said Grandpa, "perhaps we should tell Mungo what we've decided? That's if you agree, of course, Mungo, for it's up to you. I have invited you to stay with us for a week — I rather think Fanny would like to have you for company — and your aunt has agreed and then after that you will go back to Edinburgh and stay with her."

20

On the Road Again

For the first mile or so I was too busy thinking about what I'd left behind to enjoy being on the road again. We were only going to be on the road for a few miles before we caught the Edinburgh train at Pitlochry.

"I can take you in the Range Rover," Fanny's grandfather had said, "or you can cycle. I don't mind one way or the other." I think he knew which I'd choose.

"I should hope so," said Gulliver, who was in a good mood now that his wheels were spinning again and his pedals turning. "I wouldn't have fancied any more of being tossed about in that Range Rover."

"You only had a mile of it before."

"That was enough."

Gulliver hadn't enjoyed his stay much at Fanny's house. I'd only taken him out twice, once on our own for about half an hour and another time with Fanny on her bike. He hadn't thought a great deal of her machine!

"Call that a bike! Hasn't even got any gears."

I'd had to hold him back going downhill and on the flat. And we had walked up hills. The chain of Fanny's bike came off twice and I'd got my hands covered in oil. Then I'd put my oily hands on Gulliver's handlebars. You can imagine what he had to say about that! He was even less pleased when I gave Fanny a shot on him, though he behaved beautifully.

"Gulliver's fantastic!" said Fanny. "I could ride to the moon on him."

I think maybe he began to change his mind slightly about her after that. When I was putting him away in the shed he mumbled, "She's not too bad. For a girl, that is."

"You are a real chauvinist pig of a bicycle, Gully. That's what my dad would call you."

"*Father!*"

"He's my dad, do you hear? And don't you forget that!"

"Anyway, he's got no right to call anyone anything."

"Why not? Just because he made a mistake!"

"It was a bad mistake, though, wasn't it? A criminal mistake."

"But he's being punished. And he's not bad, not right through, not deep down. I *know* he's not." And I didn't care any more what Billy or anyone else had to say about him. They didn't matter to me. My dad did. And I was going to go and see him as soon as I could after we got home. I'd told him I would on a picture postcard of the Perthshire hills that I bought in Mrs McWhirter's shop.

"You like my dad, don't you, Gully?"

"I guess I do. He gave me to you, after all. Though sometimes I wonder if I should like him for that!"

I rang his bell and went on ringing it until he yelled for mercy.

"Pax, pax!" he cried.

On the same day that we'd had this conversation,

Grandpa had said at lunch, "I've decided, Fanny, that it's time you had a new bicycle. How would you like one for your birthday?"

"I'd love one! And then the next time Mungo comes to stay we can go for long rides together."

"That's what I was thinking. I hope you will come back, Mungo?"

"Oh, yes, please! And I'm going to ask my mum if Fanny can come and visit us in Edinburgh."

"I don't see any reason why she shouldn't, do you, Mrs Fyffe?"

"It would make a nice change for her. I'm very fond of Edinburgh myself, for a day or two at any rate. But after that the traffic gets too much for me."

There was not much traffic on the road to Pitlochry on the morning of our departure but once we hit the A9 there would be a lot more.

"Thank goodness we're getting a semi-decent ride at last," said Gulliver, "without any old bicycle crocks to hold us back!"

"Keep into the edge, now," Mrs Fyffe had cautioned me. "Ride carefully."

"And give us a call when you get home," Grandpa had said.

They'd come out to the front porch to see me off and Fanny had walked with me down the drive.

"You'll write, won't you?" she said.

"Cross my heart!"

"And be sure to tell me about your dad. How you get on when you go to see him."

"Oh, I will! And you'll write and tell me about the house and everything?"

"Yes, everything."

Grandpa had decided to have the big house demolished.

"It'll cost money to pull it down," he said, "but it costs quite a lot just to have it sitting there. I have to pay rates on it. And the place is falling to bits anyway, what with dry rot and wet rot and it won't be long before the roof becomes unsafe."

Fanny and I had looked at one another. I knew that she was thinking the same thing as I was. What would happen to Jane when the bulldozers moved in? But we decided when we discussed it later that ghosts would have ways of coping with things like that. And perhaps if the house was destroyed Jane would then be at peace herself.

I hate saying goodbye to people. I said it quickly to Fanny.

"Goodbye, Mungo," she said.

Looking back from the end of the road, I saw her waving still, a girl in a light-coloured dress.

"Look at the colour on that hill!" said Gulliver. "Open your eyeballs, Mungo McKinnon!"

The colour was pretty fantastic, purply and pink with the deep green of the firs making patterns against it. And the birds were rattling away, giving us a cheery chorus in the woods as we passed. We were riding beside a loch now. The reflections of the trees in the water were amazing, so amazing that I almost swerved across the road.

"Watch it!" said Gulliver. "Let's get to Pitlochry in two pieces!"

It *was* good, though, to be back on the road again. And one of the best things about it was that we didn't have to worry about police cars coming up behind us.

"I tell you what," said Gulliver, "sometime, when you're older and they've all stopped fussing, let's take off on a proper journey."

"Where would you like to go?"

"I fancy going right up north, to John O'Groats, and along the north coast to Cape Wrath and down the other side."

"Wouldn't mind that myself."

"We might even let Fanny come with us."

"Are you feeling all right, Gully?"

"We *might*, I said. It depends on what kind of bike she gets."

I smiled.

"Right?" said Gulliver.

"Right!" I said and rang his bell.

JELLYBEAN

Tessa Duder

A sensitive modern novel about Geraldine, alias 'Jellybean', who leads a rather solitary life as the only child of a single parent. She's tired of having to fit in with her mother's busy schedule, but a new friend and a performance of *The Nutcracker Suite* change everything.

THE PRIESTS OF FERRIS

Maurice Gee

Susan Ferris and her cousin Nick return to the world of O, which they had saved from the evil Halfmen, only to find that O is now ruled by cruel and ruthless priests. Can they save the inhabitants of O from tyranny? An action-packed and gripping story by the author of prize-winning *The Halfmen of O*.

THE SEA IS SINGING

Rosalind Kerven

In her seaside Shetland home Tess is torn between the plight of the whales and loyalty to her father and his job on the oil rig. A haunting and thought-provoking novel.

BACK HOME

Michelle Magorian

A marvellously gripping story of an irrepressible girl's struggle to adjust to a new life. Twelve-year-old Rusty, who had been evacuated to the United States when she was seven, returns to the grey austerity of post-war Britain.

THE BEAST MASTER

Andre Norton

Spine-chilling science fiction – treachery and revenge! Hosteen Storm is a man with a mission to find and punish Brad Quade, the man who killed his father long ago on Terra, the planet where life no longer exists.

THE PRIME MINISTER'S BRAIN
Gillian Cross

The fiendish Demon Headmaster plans to gain control of No. 10 Downing Street and lure the Prime Minister into his evil clutches.

JASON BODGER AND THE PRIORY GHOST
Gene Kemp

A ghost story, both funny and exciting, about Jason, the bane of every teacher's life, who is pursued by the ghost of a little nun from the twelfth century!

HALFWAY ACROSS THE GALAXY AND TURN LEFT
Robin Klein

A humorous account of what happens to a family banished from their planet, Zygron, when they have to spend a period of exile on Earth.

SUPERGRAN TO THE RESCUE
Forrest Wilson

The punch-packing, baddie-biffing escapades of the world's No. 1 senior citizen superhero – Super Gran! Now a devastating series on ITV!

TOM TIDDLER'S GROUND
John Rowe Townsend

Vic and Brain are given an old rowing boat which leads to the unravelling of a mystery and a happy reunion of two friends. An exciting adventure story.

THE FINDING

Nina Bawden

Alex doesn't know his birthday because he was found abandoned next to Cleopatra's Needle, so instead of a birthday he celebrates his Finding. After he inherits an unexpected fortune, Alex's life suddenly becomes very exciting indeed.

RACSO AND THE RATS OF NIMH

Jane Leslie Conly

When fieldmouse Timothy Frisby rescues young Racso, the city rat, from drowning it's the beginning of a friendship and an adventure. The two are caught up in the struggle of the Rats of NIMH to save their home from destruction. A powerful sequel to *Mrs Frisby and the Rats of Nimh*.

NICOBOBINUS

Terry Jones

Nicobobinus and his friend, Rosie, find themselves involved in all sorts of intriguing adventures when they set out to find the Land of the Dragons long ago. Stunningly illustrated by Michael Foreman.

FRYING AS USUAL

Joan Lingard

When Mr Francetti breaks his leg it looks as if his fish restaurant will have to close, so Toni, Rosita and Paula decide to keep things going.

DRIFT

William Mayne

A thrilling adventure of a young boy and an Indian girl, stranded on a frozen floating island in the North American wilderness.

COME SING, JIMMY JO

Katherine Paterson

An absorbing story about eleven-year-old Jimmy Jo's rise to stardom and the problem of coping with fame.